THE MAGIC INK

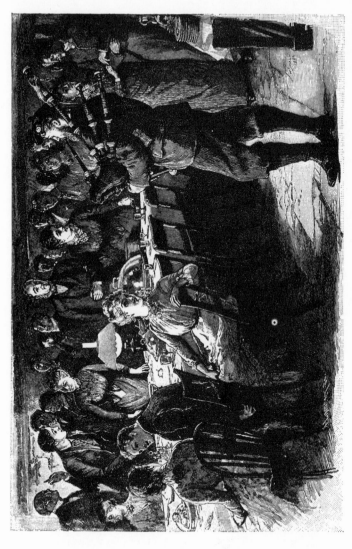

" AND WHEN HECTOR MAC INTYRE . . HAD PLAYED THE PEOPLE IN "

[Page 83

THE MAGIC INK

AND OTHER STORIES

BY

WILLIAM BLACK

ILLUSTRATED

Short Story Index

BOOKS FOR LIBRARIES PRESS
FREEPORT, NEW YORK

First Published 1892
Reprinted 1972

INTERNATIONAL STANDARD BOOK NUMBER:
0-8369-4096-2

LIBRARY OF CONGRESS CATALOG CARD NUMBER:
79-37537

PRINTED IN THE UNITED STATES OF AMERICA
BY
NEW WORLD BOOK MANUFACTURING CO., INC.
HALLANDALE, FLORIDA 33009

CONTENTS

PAGE

THE MAGIC INK, ... 1

A HALLOWE'EN WRAITH, ... 75

NANCIEBEL: A TALE OF STRATFORD-ON-AVON, . . . 117

ILLUSTRATIONS.

"AND WHEN HECTOR MAC INTYRE . . . HAD PLAYED
      THE PEOPLE IN" . . . . *Frontispiece*

"FROM OUT OF THE DUSK OF THE WALL" . . . *Facing page* 78

"I WILL SEARCH MY POCKETS" . . . .   "   82

"FLORA AND HE SITTING TOGETHER IN THE STERN
      OF THE BOAT, AND ALL OF THEM SINGING THE
      'FEAR A BHATA'" . . . .   "   102

"SHE TRIED TO LIFT HER WASTED HAND TO MEET
      HIS" . . . .   "   114

"THE TWO FIGURES WERE WELL WRAPPED UP, FOR
      THE NIGHT WAS COLD" . . . .   "   120

THE MAGIC INK

THE MAGIC INK

CHAPTER I

THE ROBBERY

At the very busiest hour of the afternoon a young man of about one-and-twenty was making his way along the crowded thoroughfare of the Strand, carrying in his hand a satchel that had stamped on it in gold letters, "Cripps' Bank." He was rather a good-looking young fellow, with pale, refined features, a sensitive mouth, jet-black hair, and mild, contemplative gray eyes. Eyes were meant for seeing; but sometimes they refuse to perform their office; at this precise moment, for example, this young bank-clerk beheld nothing of St. Clement's Church, nor of the frontage of the Law Courts, nor yet of the fearful wild-fowl that marks the site of Temple Bar. What he did see before him—here in the heart of the great commercial centre of the world—was a dream-picture of a small slate-quarrying village in the west of Wales, its rows

of cottages, its terraced black cliffs, its squalid
little harbor, and the ruffled blue sea beyond.
And if the schoolmaster's daughter—Miss Winifred—she of the raven hair, and the violet eyes,
and the pleasant smile—were to come along by
those cottages, and past the Wesleyan chapel,
and go away up into the wooded vale running
inland, so that she might secure a perfect solitude in which to read her last letter from London? Llanly is a commonplace little hamlet;
and the slate-quarries are not picturesque; but
youth and love combined can throw a mystic
glamour over anything. What was this song
that was running through his head? He had
got the words, such as they were, scribbled out
all right; and now he was seeking for an air for
them—something pensive and wistful, and yet
not too sad either:

Sweet Winnie Davies, down by the sea,
Sweet Winnie Davies, do you still think of me?
Do you think of the long days you and I together
Went wandering by Llanly in the fair summer weather?

So the words began; but they were of less importance; it was the setting of them—to some
air worthy of sweet Winnie Davies herself—that
more particularly claimed his attention. For
this young Welshman, his Celtic nature all compact of imagination, and poetry, and romantic

sympathy and sentiment, was chiefly a musician; his tentative performances had been in that sphere; there also lay his far-reaching hopes. That he was also a bank-clerk may be ascribed to the irony of fate; but he did not complain; and sweet Winnie Davies had considered him a very sensible young man in accepting this post when it was offered him, seeing that he was anxious above all things to get to London. As to whether he carried with him a conductor's bâton in his knapsack, who was to foresee?

When this young Arthur Hughes reached the offices of the Temple Bar Branch of the London and Westminster Bank, he entered by the heavily-swinging doors, and approached the counter. There were a good many people coming and going; the clerks at the various desks were occupied. Young Hughes perceived that he would have to wait his turn before he could get his business transacted, so he placed his satchel on the counter beside him, and remained absently attentive, if the phrase is permissible. There is a hushed somnolence about the atmosphere of a bank, a drowsy whispering of pens and shuffling of feet, that invites to contemplation when one has nothing to do but wait. And when one has been, but a few seconds before (if only dream-wise), in a little Welsh village— looking at the harbor, and the quarries, and the cottages, and the slim little figure of the school-master's daughter—it is perhaps easy to return thither. There are times and seasons when the imagination becomes a powerful necromancer; hey, presto! and the bare walls of this place of business suddenly vanish, and in their stead there stands revealed once more that Welsh landscape—the cliffs and woods, the scattered cottages, the breadth of sea beyond. But it is with that solitary figure he is wholly concerned; he follows her with entranced eyes, watching every grace and charm of movement, and glad that the sunlight is around her. Nor does she seem at all downcast, notwithstanding that her sweetheart is so far away. On the contrary, there is an abundant cheerfulness in her expression; her step is free and light; perhaps she is singing to herself—only the immeasurable distance deadens the sound. And now, what is this? She pauses in her aimless stroll; she turns and looks along the road, as if to make sure there is no one in sight; then she produces from her pocket a small hand-mirror, and proceeds to scrutinize her appearance in it. And a very pretty picture she undoubtedly finds there —the black eyelashes and violet eyes, the clear and fresh complexion, the waving black hair; and is her vanity so great that she must needs smile and look pleased, and even begin to talk to herself? Arthur Hughes knows better. It is not vanity—nor anything like vanity. He can remember how she wrote to him shortly after his coming to London:

"Will you be desperately shocked, dear Arthur, if I tell you that I have found a new companion? But wait a moment—don't be alarmed!— wait a moment, and I will explain. The fact is, I found myself so lonely after you left that I was absolutely driven to do something; and do you know what I did?—I cut myself in two. Yes; I divided myself into two persons, my Ordinary Self and my Other Self; and I find the system works admirably. For my Ordinary Self is a most commonplace, uninteresting, useless kind of creature—indeed, indeed, 'tis too true— living a humdrum, monotonous, worthless life, with a sigh now and again for certain things that are past, and another sigh for other things that are far away in the future; but my Other Self—ah, that is different!—my Other Self is the young lady that Arthur praised, and petted, and teased, and made much of: and she, I can tell you, is entitled to some consideration! And now, when my Ordinary Self takes my Other Self out for a walk, don't you understand that I have some right to be proud of my companion? I have got a little pocket-mirror, Arthur; I go away up the Megan road; I take it out; and then the Ordinary Winnie says 'Good-morning!' to the other Winnie.

"'Good-morning, Miss Other One; let me see how you look. It is of no consequence how *I* look. *My* appearance is of not the least consequence to any one; but *you*—you whom Arthur imagined into existence—it is of the utmost importance that you should be trim and neat and nice, for you know he is *very* particular. Yes—pretty well—not so bad—the sea-shell brooch on the black velvet band is what he approved. The saffron frill might be a little broader; attend to that. Now, go on, and tell me all the things he has said about you.'

"'All of them?' says my Other Self. 'Well, he has called me good, and sweet, and kind, and charming, and good-tempered, and clever, and affectionate, and true, and tender, and wonderful, and delightful——'

"'It is not surprising you should give yourself airs!'

"'——and stupid, and silly, and perverse, and ill-natured, and cross, and unyielding, and unjust, and quarrelsome, and obstinate——'

"'Not so much to boast of, after all!' says my Ordinary Self. 'But now let me hear some of the things you have said about him, to himself, or to yourself, or to other people.'

"'Oh, no, you don't!' says my Other Self,

laughing at me from the mirror. 'Telling's telling. You might go away and write it all down; and send it over to London; and then there would be such an exhibition of vanity as was never seen in the world before. It wouldn't be at all wholesome. You often say things you don't quite mean; and it isn't safe to put them down on paper; at the same time, if Arthur were to appear here just now—well—I should most likely ask *you* to go away—*you* would not be wanted here at all—and then, if he and I were left together, then I might say some of those things over again. But to have them written down—no, thank you!'

"So, you see, dear Arthur, the companion I have invented—or, rather, whom you imagined into existence for me—is not at all monotonously civil and acquiescent; sometimes we have dreadful quarrels; but in such cases my Ordinary Self is easily triumphant; my Ordinary Self claps the mirror into her pocket—and then walks home alone."

Thus it was that Arthur Hughes, standing in the London and Westminster Bank, and gazing through the opaque walls at that distant dreamland, knew it was no personal vanity that prompted Winnie Davies to carry a little handglass with her on her solitary wanderings. No, it was rather a pretty fancy, that lent charm and

1*

piquancy to many a letter; for sometimes, if the truth must be told, the Ordinary Winnie considerately allowed the Other Winnie to have far the larger part of the conversation, she merely acting the part of reporter, and not holding herself responsible when any dark and mysterious secrets had to be confessed.

It was at this moment that some one touched Arthur Hughes' arm; instantly the dream-picture (that had been before his eyes for perhaps not more than three seconds or so) disappeared: he was again in the Strand.

"I beg your pardon," said a voice close to him, "but can you direct me to the London and Counties Bank?"

Naturally he faced round to see who the questioner was. He found before him a tall, meagre, gray-complexioned man, with an aquiline nose, steely eyes, and a "goatee;" and he was just about to give the desired information when some curious instinct caused him to turn again, to see that his hand-bag was safe. It was gone! In that brief instant it had been snatched away—no doubt by a confederate of the American-looking stranger. But that was not what Arthur Hughes understood just then; he thought of neither why nor wherefore; blank horror had fallen over him; he seemed to be drowning and choking, and to have lost the power of speech. The

satchel—and its £7,560 belonging to his employers—vanished into air: it was as if he had
been dealt some violent blow, depriving him of
reason.   His haggard eyes stared up and down;
the world around him appeared strangely empty;
and then, as the clerk on the other side of the
counter, seeing that something was wrong, asked
him a question, he managed to stammer out,
in panting accents:

"My bag—there were £7,560 in bank-notes
in it—belonging to Cripps'—I had it a moment
ago——"

The next instant the truth flashed in upon
him: he had been robbed—and the tall man who
had touched him on the arm, to distract his attention, was one of the thieves.   Blindly and
wildly he made for the swinging-door and rushed
into the street.   He could easily recognize the
tall man; the confederates could not be far away;
was there not yet a frantic chance of recovery?
But, alas! what was this that confronted him—
this endless surging sea of human beings into
which those two had disappeared?   He ran this
way and that; he hurriedly searched the hall of
the Law Courts opposite; he glanced breathlessly in at the bars of the neighboring taverns—
but with an ever-increasing and terrible consciousness that his pursuit was hopeless, that already the thieves were well away with their

booty, and that a calamity too awful to be calcu-
lated or even thought of had befallen him. It
had all happened so rapidly as to be quite incredible. He kept trying to assure himself that
it was impossible. Why, only a few minutes
ago he had nothing more important to think of
than the setting of a song for Winifred Davies.
The hand-bag must be somewhere—somewhere
near: there may have been a mistake. And so
he went quickly back to the bank.

The cashier to whom he had formerly spoken
was engaged; but in his agony of haste he made
bold to interrupt.

"I beg your pardon," he said breathlessly,
"but—but have you seen anything yet of my
bag? I—I had it only a few moments ago—
here—here on this counter——"

The cashier looked up from his checks.

"Your bag? No. Have you lost it?"

"It must have been stolen—only a few moments ago!" he exclaimed; "here—just where
I am standing. I set it on the counter—some
one spoke to me, and I turned for a moment.
It cannot be in the bank, then? They must
have stolen it!"

"If that is so," said the cashier, "you'd better
jump into a hansom and drive along to Scotland
Yard."

"But they cannot have gone far——"

He rushed again into the street, and with distracted eyes looked everywhere around, and looked in vain: the dread thing was that this moving phantasmagoria was full of features, but no one of them of any import to him. The pavements showed him nothing; the cab-rank showed him nothing; the passing omnibuses took no heed of him. He hurried hither and thither, searching the many places he had searched a few moments before—the bars of the adjacent taverns, the entrance to the Law Courts, and what-not; but nowhere could he find any one resembling the man who had asked him for the whereabouts of the London and Counties.· And at last conviction and despair confronted him, and would not be denied. The money was gone. No one would believe the improbable tale he would have to tell of the manner of its disappearance. There would be a prosecution—conviction —a prison; disgrace would fall on his old father, the white-haired Wesleyan minister, whose chief pride in life was his only son. And as for Winifred Davies? Well, she had made many promises before he left Llanly, but she never undertook to correspond with a jail-bird.

Now, if in this sudden and terrible crisis Arthur Hughes had managed to keep his wits about him, he would have perceived that the best, the only, thing for him to do, was to go straight

away back to Cripps', tell the officials of the bank
(whether they believed him or not) precisely
what had occurred, and let them place the whole
matter at once in the hands of the police. But
this young man was of a highly nervous, sensitive, high-strung temperament; his imagination
magnified dangers, and even created them; and,
above all, it was not so much of himself as of
those nearest and dearest to him that he was
now thinking, so far as he was able to think.
And in truth he was not able to think very
clearly. Dazed, bewildered, desperate, to him
this roaring thoroughfare of the Strand was a
dreadful and hideous place; the noise of the
cabs and carriages, the wagons and omnibuses,
seemed to stupefy him; he was driven to go
elsewhere for some brief space of self-commun-
ion. And so, hardly knowing what he did, he
turned into one of the narrow thoroughfares
leading down to the Thames embankment: there
he would find quietude, and a chance of realizing
to himself what this ghastly thing was that had
just happened, and what its consequences were
likely to be.

But here a singular and unexpected little incident occurred, that he afterward, in less distracted moments, was able to recall. Some
short distance down the narrow street the way
was blocked, or nearly blocked, by a number of

vans being loaded; indeed, one of these was
nearly putting a summary end to this young
man's troubles, for, being backed on to the pavement, it swung round just as he was passing,
and was like to have pinned him against the
wall. More by quick instinct than by conscious
effort he managed to avoid it; but in doing so he
ran full tilt against a stranger, whom he knocked
over. He was very sorry. He raised the man up.
He did not notice the swift malevolent glance
of the two dull black eyes of this little yellow-
skinned person, nor yet the change to a fawning
obsequiousness that almost instantly came over
the man's manner. The street was muddy after
rain; this foreigner—Malay, Chinese, Hindoo,
whatever he was—took out a handkerchief, and
began to clean his clothes after a fashion.

"I'm very sorry," Arthur Hughes said.
"The man in charge of the van did not call out
until it was too late—I did not see you were on
the other side—I'm exceedingly sorry——"

But the baleful fire had vanished from those
small, dull black eyes.

"Oh, me solly too if you solly," said the little
foreigner, regarding the young man. "We
make flends now. Me show you we make
flends; me give you little plesent. See!"

It was a small ink-bottle he produced—an or-
dinary-looking thing.

"Take it—yes, yes, make flends," he said. "Make flends! Me solly if you solly. English good people—kind people."

Well, in other circumstances, Arthur Hughes would doubtless have declined to take an ink-bottle or any similar thing from an entire stranger encountered accidentally in the streets of London; but in his present tragic case he was quite indifferent. He was bewildered; he did not understand; only, the man seemed anxious he should accept the little present; and it was a token of good-will from one whom he had unintentionally injured. So, hardly looking at it, and thinking nothing of it, he accepted it, put it in his pocket, thanked the Eastern-looking person, and blindly went on his way. What happened to him in the matter of small trifles was of little moment now.

Down on the embankment, near to one of the stations on the Underground Railway, he saw a policeman; and he regarded him with a strange sensation of fear. There was another man driving a mud-sweeping machine; and him he envied with a bitter heart.

"How little you know of your own happiness!" he was saying, almost in reproach. "Perched up there, you are as proud as any king on any throne. You have nothing to dread. The law cannot touch you. Your conscience is clear.

You might be singing for very joy if you only knew."

For this hypersensitive young man, in the first shock of his alarm and consternation, had come to regard himself as being to all intents and purposes a criminal. He was convinced that the people at the bank—and still more the people at Scotland Yard—would not for a moment believe his tale of the two unknown persons who had spirited away his satchel; they would assume—and especially the people at Scotland Yard would assume—that he had secreted the money for his own uses and invented this cock-and-bull story about the mysterious thieves. Nor did he perceive that he was at this moment doing his very best to lend color to such a charge. He was putting himself into the position of an absconding clerk. Had he gone boldly back to the bank, told his story, and challenged inquiry, the situation would no doubt have been very unpleasant for a time, but probably no harm would have come to him in the end. But in the overwhelming dismay that fell upon him on his discovering his loss, going back to the bank seemed to him to mean nothing else than being confronted with detectives—arrest—trial—perhaps a prison. A prison! Even now, as he wandered, stunned and demented, along the embankment, he began with a morbid vivid-

ness to recall such descriptions of prison-life as
he had read. Formerly it used to be rather a
jolly life—hob-nobbing with friendly turnkeys
—sending out for further measures of claret—
receiving relatives and acquaintances and borrow-
ing money from them—throwing dice and playing cards—anything to pass the time. Perhaps
that condition of affairs was all over now; but
whether or not was of little consequence to him;
there would be for him but the one result of his
going to prison—he would never lift up his head
again. His conscience might assure him he was
innocent; his friends might pity and forgive;
but once the iron had entered his soul, for him
there would be no recovery, no restoration to
life. And the venerable old minister who had
lived all these years in the love and respect and
affection of his flock—for him to have his white
head brought down to the dust: it was too piteous to think of. Winnie Davies: but Winnie
Davies was young, and pretty, and fascinating;
a few years would go by; new springs and sum-
mers would come to her, with the thrushes singing in the evening woods, and a lover walking
by her side, linking his arm with hers. And if
in after-times she should ever think of a former
lover—of one who had gone away to London to
do great things for her sake—it would be with
anger, it would be without consideration: why

had he brought shame upon her in the days of her maidenhood?

He was a sensitive lad: in spite of himself tears rose to his eyes.

"Father—Winnie," he murmured to himself, "you need not fear. It will not come to that. There must be some other way."

There *was* another way, as it seemed to his unhinged and distracted mind: a way sombre and dark, but sure. All the forces of Scotland Yard combined could not entrap, or prosecute, or hale to prison, one who had slipped quietly and unseen into the deeps of the sea. No telegraphing to foreign ports could secure the arrest of him whose last adieu to the world was a secret confided to the night, and the stars, and the lone Atlantic.

"Do not be afraid, father," he said inwardly, amid all those wild and storm-tossed emotions that were now being narrowed down to one stern resolve. "There will be no trial. There will be no reading of newspaper reports—no whisperings among the members of the congregation. Do not be afraid, Winnie: no shame shall come to you through me. If there had been a prosecution, I think you would have believed me innocent, whatever happened; but there will be no prosecution. Those I left behind me in Llanly will have no cause to hang their heads

on my account.   What becomes of me is nothing."

And this that he was about to give up—to save
his dear ones from scorn?   Well, youth is naturally tenacious of life; it takes little heed of
the pains and struggles and rebuffs involved in
its own eager aspirations and ambitions; there
is the joy of pressing forward, to see what the
world has in store, to act one's part, to earn the
quiet of old age and retrospect.   Moreover, in
his case there were other and more idyllic visions, with Winifred Davies as their central figure.
These were harder to abandon.   He thought of
by-gone days; of long walks by sea and shore, he
and she together; of murmured confessions with
downcast lashes; of eyes upturned to his, full of
love, and hope, and pride.   For who was it that
had been most eager to prophesy great things of
his going to London?   Who had boldly declared
that his "Cadwallon's Army-Call" had more of
fire in it, had a more martial and stately tread, than
even the famous "Forth to the Battle," the *Rhy-
felgyrch Cadpen Morgan*, the war-march of Morgan
of Morganog?   Who had sung his "Bells of
Llanly" to the school children at their annual
treat, and had maintained, in public hearing, that
in her opinion it was more touching and sympathetic, more characteristically Welsh, than even
the "Bells of Aberdovey?"   Nay, had she not

gone further, and in wistful confidences to himself talked of the Crystal Palace, and of a young conductor standing in front of the great attentive choir, and of a Welsh girl seated among the audience, and saying to herself (while trembling a little), "Ah! now, you English people will hear something. Wales has sent you many musicians: judge now, by this Army-Call of Cadwallon, whether another has not been added to the list. And it was I who urged him to go away from Llanly and try his fortune in the great city—though the parting was cruel enough."

Yes; it was much to give up—life, love, ambition; but he could see no alternative. The only thing to do now was to guard against his friends in Llanly forming any suspicion as to the manner of his disappearance. He would write a letter to his father, another to Winifred, and another to Mr. Cyrus Brangwyn—a junior partner in Cripps', who had interested himself in the young man's behalf; and in these he would give such plausible explanations as he could invent. Then a quick vanishing—and silence. Black night and the Atlantic would hold his secret; his troubles would be peacefully over; and there would be no finger of scorn uplifted against those whom he had left behind him in the distant little Welsh village, the home of his youth.

CHAPTER II

THE WRITING OF THE LETTERS

THUS it was that his first frantic apprehensions were succeeded by a period of calm—the calm of resignation rather than despair. For he did not pity himself in the least; indeed, he was not thinking of himself at all. A great calamity had occurred—how, he was almost yet too bewildered to know; but his first and sole care was to shield from its consequences those dear ones whose welfare, whose happiness, whose good name, were of more concern to him than his own life. Nay, even now, in the dull and dazed condition into which he had fallen, his mind was occupied with but the one idea—to frame such excuses for his going away as would cause them neither alarm nor grief. His subsequent silence they would no doubt explain to themselves somehow or another. The old man would say: "My boy has gone away to the colonies, to seek his fortune; and he is proud; we shall not hear from him, perhaps, until he can announce to us that he has succeeded." And Winnie Davies? She would wonder for a time. Then she would grow indignant and resentful. Then her eyes— as the eyes of a young maiden are apt to do—

22

would begin to rove; recollections, memories would become gradually obliterated; she would take it that in those distant climes he had forgotten all about her and the little Welsh village; she would feel herself justified in choosing another mate.

Sweet Winnie Davies, down by the sea,
Sweet Winne Davies, do you still think of me?
Do you think of the long days you and I together
Went wandering by Llanly in the fair summer weather?

—that was all very well as a bit of idle rhyme; but the way of the world was the way of the world; a young maiden's imaginative fancies are soon free to grace and adorn a new-comer. Indeed, what else could he wish for her? For her, long years of happiness and calm content: for him, oblivion—and a nameless ocean grave.

Plunged in these sombre reveries, he had left the embankment, crossed the river, and was now in the Blackfriars Road. He had taken this route mechanically, it being part of his usual homeward way; but he had no intention of returning to his lodgings in the Kennington Park Road; would there not be a detective hovering about—perhaps with a warrant of arrest in his hand? No; his immediate object was to get those three letters written; and so, after some little hesitation, he entered a dingy-looking coffee-shop. He glanced timidly and furtively around; he knew he had entered on false pretences; it was neither food nor drink that was in his mind. Well, there seemed to be nobody in this dusky place except a stout woman—probably the proprietress—who was seated behind a counter at the farther end; but presently there emerged from some mysterious recess a shabbily-dressed man in black who was doubtless the waiter. A poor-looking creature he was, with a pale and puffy face that suggested gin; and yet Arthur Hughes, so unstrung were his nerves, had some vague desire to propitiate this person: he hoped he would not stare too curiously, even with those dull eyes.

"I should like some tea and a roll, if you please," said Hughes, with averted look (would the man guess that he wanted neither tea nor roll?).

The waiter—without any "Yes, sir"—was perfunctorily turning away to order these things, when Hughes ventured to address him again.

"Would you mind getting me some writing-paper in the mean time?"

"How many sheets?" the waiter responded, apathetically: he seemed to take no interest whatever in this visitor, who need not have been so alarmed about awakening suspicion.

"Three, I think, will do—and three envelopes, if you please."

Then of a sudden it occurred to him that he could at least spare the waiter the bother of fetching pen and ink: had he not with him the bottle that had just been given him by the foreigner whom he had accidentally thrown into the mud?—while there was a pen in combination with his pocket-pencil.

"You needn't trouble about pen and ink," he said, quite humbly; "I have them with me."

And then he turned into a corner, and took his seat on a bench that had a narrow table in front of it. Mechanically he pulled out his pocket-pen and opened it; mechanically he brought forth from his pocket the little phial: his head was so crowded with memories and strange imaginings that he hardly knew what he was doing. It was without curiosity that he opened the small bottle—the cork giving way easily: he may have noticed that the ink emitted a pungent and unusual odor, and yet he paid no particular attention to the fact. Indeed, he did not stay to consider how odd it was that the Eastern-looking person should have insisted on making him a present in return for an injury, however unintentional the injury may have been: it was of other things he was thinking. The waiter fetched the paper and envelopes. The pen and ink were ready. And now he set to work to construct a cloak under cover of which

2

he might escape into blackness and the unknown.

The first letter was to the junior partner in
Cripps' who had procured for him a situation
in the bank. This Mr. Cyrus Brangwyn was on
a walking-tour in Wales when he chanced to
make Arthur Hughes' acquaintance; had been
much struck by the young man's manner, his
intelligence, his sympathetic nature; and on
further discovering young Hughes' eager desire
to get to London, he had offered to use his influence to procure him a post, however minor a
one, in Cripps'. Hughes, who was merely an
assistant clerk at the Llanly slate-works, gladly
accepted the offer: to be in London was the
main point, no matter in what capacity. London, with its Albert Halls and St. James' Halls,
its opera-houses and Crystal Palace—that was
the Mecca of this young man's mind; he did not
care in what guise he might travel thither, nor
by what modest means he might maintain himself there, so long as he was enabled to live in
the enchanted capital that drew the great ones
of the music-world from all parts of the earth.
Then there came a morning at Llanly, a dull,
gray, bitterly cold winter's morning. The old
omnibus was drawn up in front of the Pembroke
Arms, getting in its freight for the railway station some dozen miles off. The venerable,

white-headed minister was here, talking his grave fashion to this one and that of the by-standers. Here, likewise, was Winnie Davies—tearful—laughing—courageous—petulant. Why would he not let her drive with him to the station? If it would be lonely for her coming back, it would be as lonely for him in the cold third-class carriage journeying on to London. Would he write as often as he had promised? No, she knew he would not. He was to be sure to ask for a foot-warmer at the station. He was to be sure to go and hear Santley sing at the Crystal Palace, and to send her a long letter about it. And, therewithal, as the driver was now mount-ing the box, she drew from her pocket a volu-minous neckerchief of pale pink silk, and this parting gift she would herself wrap round his throat. Then the commonplaces of good-by; and other farewells—not so commonplace—spoken by eyes half-dimmed and piteous. The brake is removed; the lumbering omnibus moves off; there is a fluttering of handkerchiefs and long last looks: Arthur Hughes is away to Lon-don, in quest of fame and fortune, and Winnie, "sweet Winnie Davies," walks silently back by the side of the minister, hardly knowing that he is doing his best, in his grave and kindly fash-ion, to cheer her.

"To Cyrus Brangwyn, Esq., Cripps' Bank, Strand"—this was the letter he wrote and addressed, sitting in a corner of the dingy coffee-house—"Dear Sir:—I am sorry to have to tell you that this afternoon I lost my satchel containing £7,560 belonging to the bank, and that I am quite powerless to give you any information that might lead to the recovery of the same. I cannot explain how the satchel was taken, nor can I describe the thieves; but the numbers of the notes are known to the bank, and by advertising I suppose they can be stopped, at least the large ones, which are not easily negotiable. As for the smaller notes which the thieves may be able to put in circulation, I regret that I am not in a position to make good the loss to the bank; but I am leaving this country; and if I should ever find it possible to refund the money, you may be sure I will do so. If you think it necessary to make any inquiries about me, I ask you only for one thing—not to make inquiries at Llanly. I assure you it is not there I am going. I would give you my word of honor; but unhappily, in the position I find myself placed in—and the suspicion naturally attaching to it—you might not be inclined to accept that as of any value. However, what I tell you is true: I am *not* going to Llanly; and any one making inquiries there would only give pain to innocent people, and would gain no information about me. I have to thank you, dear Mr. Brangwyn, for all the kindness you have shown me since I came to London, though I am sorry I ever did come. If I ever return to London, it will be to restore the money to the bank.

> "Yours very faithfully,
> "ARTHUR HUGHES."

A sudden sound startled him: a boy in the street was bawling out the name of an evening journal. And like a knife the thought flashed through his brain: what if his scheme should fail? He seemed to see before him the contents-bill of one of those evening newspapers—large lines staring at him—"Charge of Robbing a Bank—Proceedings this Day." And would not a summarized report be at once telegraphed down to Wales? Who would be the first to hear the story—in the quiet little village?

And then again he strove to reassure himself. His scheme could not fail—there was no possibility of its failing—once he was on board the big steamer that would carry him out into the night. A noiseless slipping over into the dark and unknown waters—and no writ or warrant could reach him then. There could be no charge brought against one who had ceased to exist; there would be no evidence, no witnesses, no public trial, no report to be telegraphed down to Wales. There remained only to make these last sad preparations.

But meanwhile that sudden sound had also startled the pallid-faced waiter; it seemed to arouse him out of his dull lethargy. He cast a surreptitious glance toward his mistress, who appeared to have fallen asleep: then quickly and stealthily he went to the door. He was gone for only a second or two; when he returned, he had an evening paper in his hand; and a marvellous change had come over his features—he was all eagerness and suppressed excitement.

"Archipelago!" he said, in a confidential whisper, to Arthur Hughes.

The young man looked up, dazed; he did not understand.

"What is it?"

"The Rose Plate—Newmarket——"

And even yet he did not seem to comprehend.

"It was fifteen to eight against; I've made my little bit this time," said the waiter, who could not altogether conceal his triumph, though he spoke guardedly.

"Oh, a race, do you mean!"

"Well, sir, if we didn't pick out a winner now and again, we'd never get along—just to keep one's heart up like. They tell me that Red Star is a moral for the Cambridgeshire——"

But at this juncture the mistress of the place made some movement, and the waiter sneaked off, and began to apply his napkin to one of the tables. Arthur Hughes looked after him.

"Man, man," he said to himself, "have you no thought of the terrible things around you in the world that you can occupy yourself with such trifles? And yet, why not? What better than to think of nothing from day to day but the constant and common routine, with this little variety of interest? One morning must be just like another morning, one night like another night, quiet and ordinary; nothing haunting you, nothing to dread. I wonder if you know how well off you are—I wonder if you know what a priceless blessing it is to be without care?"

And therewithal, and heavily-hearted enough, he turned once more to his series of farewells. It was to his father that he would now write.

"DEAR FATHER:—You know with what aspirations I came to London. But after some study of the musical world, from the outside, of course, I find that the openings for a young composer, unless he is of extraordinary ability, or has powerful friends, are few indeed. On the other hand, promotion in a London bank is by slow steps; the increase of salary small; and little opportunity given for one's personal endeavors.

So I have resolved to leave England, and seek some wider and freer sphere. You must not be alarmed, or fret, if you do not hear from me for some time; for my plans are as yet vague; and I may wander far before coming to a halt. Be kind to Winnie. Even if you do not hear from me for a very long time, do not worry on my account.

"Your affectionate son,

"ARTHUR HUGHES."

These two letters had been comparatively easy to write. But when he came to the message he must send to Winnie Davies, he paused. A haggard and drawn look came over his face; it was as if the hand of death were already upon him; and as if this were the farewell dooming her to widowhood. And then a strange exaltation of self-sacrifice entered his heart. If he were parting with her, and yielding her to some one else, he would see that those days of her widowhood should be brief and be not embittered by any useless sorrow. He would make it easy for her to forget him; he would challenge her wounded pride to help. For what more possible than that a young man, far away from his native village and its associations, and plunged into this roaring city, should have allowed his wandering inclinations to stray from the sweetheart of his youth and fix themselves on some one nearer at hand? The briefest hint would be enough. Winnie Davies was proud; she would seek no further correspondence; his silence thereafter would be no trouble to her hurt and indignant spirit. And so, with rather bloodless lips, he began to write:

"Dear Miss Winifred—" He stopped and looked. "Dear Miss Winifred." That was the way he used to address her in the remote days when her father and she first came to Llanly, and when she became a member of the village choir. But in those days "Dear Miss Winifred" meant respect and a timid appeal for friendship; whereas now the phrase was meant to wound and insult. Never mind; the pang would be but temporary—and the days of her widowhood would have no vain longings and regrets attached.

"Dear Miss Winifred:—What I have to say may pain you for the moment, but it is better for us both that it should be said at once and done with. I am afraid you were wiser than I when you hinted that our engagement was somewhat premature, and therefore involving risk. And if I admit that, living very much alone in London, and craving for sympathy as is natural

2*

with a solitary stranger in a large town, I have
met with some one else whose attractions have
convinced me that the engagement between you
and me was a mistake from the beginning——"

He paused again, and regarded these lines.
The poor conventional phrases, the cold arti-
ficiality of tone; who could have imagined that
each word went like a dagger through his heart?
And indeed he could not go on. He was about
to die; it was not thus he could send a last message to Winnie Davies. He might have to conceal much from her; he would have to let her
believe that some day or other he might return;
but he could not, even in the short time that was
now left to him of life, bear the thought that all
through the long years to come she would regard him with scorn and disdain as a false friend
and perjured lover. It was too much for him to
demand of himself. So he tore up that sheet of
paper, and began again—but still with caution
and self-control dominating his brain and trying
to still the almost suffocating pulses of heart:

"DEAREST WINNIE:—I have something to tell
you which may surprise you, but it is not meant
to cause you any distress. It is merely that I
am not quite satisfied with my position in London; and that I am going away. I have nothing

to complain of as against any one; but there are circumstances which seem to call me away from London; and I am sure it will be better for us all in the end. You will say I ought to have come down to Llanly to bid you good-by; and you may be sure I do not forget your kindness in getting up that bitterly cold morning, nor yet all the things your eyes said after I was on the top of the coach and you could no longer speak. But the world is full of changes and disappointments; and if I do not run down to Llanly now to see you again, it is because there are urgent reasons against it. I wish you would often go over to see my father; he is very lonely by himself in the house, and you know how fond he is of you. If you ever speak of me don't be vexed that I have left you in a kind of uncertainty; and you must always remember this, *that no news is good news.* And now, dearest Winnie, good-by, and God bless you! Do not write to me—I am going away from London.   ARTHUR."

And therewith he corked up the little bottle of oddly-scented ink and put it in his pocket again along with his pen; he paid for the tea and roll which he had not touched; he purchased some stamps for the letters, and left the coffee-house, wandering out alone into the wide wilderness of London.

And now he was free to go; his affairs in this world were all finished up; there was nothing left for him but to slip quietly away out of the knowledge of men, so that his beloved ones should have no suspicion. But all of a sudden a blunt matter of fact interposed here, as he stood hesitating and absent-minded in the Blackfriars Road. He had only a few shillings in his pocket. How was he to purchase a passage in any Canadian or American steamer, in order that on some dark night he might disappear into the voiceless grave of the Atlantic? He had, it is true—apart from the bulk of his savings, which were deposited in the Llanly bank—a few sovereigns at home in his lodgings; but even if these were sufficient to secure a berth (as to which he had no precise information), how could he return to fetch them? Already, he vaguely surmised, the place was being watched. Detectives were after the absconding clerk. Nay, even now, when he had formed no definite plans at all, he had unconsciously turned toward the heart of the great city, and was slowly and impassively making for Blackfriars Bridge again. How happy— how careless—were those people he saw around him! The big draymen were cracking jokes as they lowered barrels into the public-house cellars. The rubicund driver of an omnibus raised his whip in salutation to the driver of a butcher's cart, who responded in gay fashion. Even a blind beggar, chanting his unheeded stave, seemed content; by and by, with a few pence in his pocket, he would creep away home to the common lodging-house, to his pipe and his cronies, sufficiently well satisfied with such poor and small share of the world as had been accorded him. How gladly would this hapless young man have exchanged positions with any one of these, had not a tragic destiny encompassed him! But for him there was no escape. Indeed, he wished for no escape. It was not about himself he was concerned. How many years would it be before Winnie Davies would quite abandon all hope of hearing from him— would choose out another lover—would go round by the quay, and through the town, and up the vale, to meet him, singing lightly to herself the while "Cadair Idris," or "The Watching of the Wheat?" For he hoped, and wished, for no impossible things in the way of constancy. Perhaps, after all, Winnie Davies might sometimes think of him; and if she did, it would not be as of a jail-bird. He would make sure of that.

He wandered on. The black world of London was now ablaze with points of yellow fire; cabs and carriages were driving to the theatres; the restaurants showed wide doors. He drew away toward the east; and as the slow hours

passed there was greater darkness here and loneliness.   A considerable traffic still poured down
toward London Bridge; but about the Exchange,
and Cornhill, and Gracechurch Street, fewer and
fewer persons were to be met.   Why had he
come hither?   Because he had a dim recollection that in Fenchurch Street was the station
for Tilbury and Tilbury Docks; and he knew
that from thence went great steamers out into
the unknown seas which were his goal.   It was
a short railway journey; so far at least he could
get; and once down there at the docks, who
could tell what happy accident might bring him
to his desire?   So he idly patrolled these dark
and silent thoroughfares, as hour after hour
went by—rather avoiding this or that passing
policeman, whose suspicious glance he knew was
directed toward him.

Then, with the coming of the gray light of the
dawn, and while the side-thoroughfares were
as yet deserted—especially Fenchurch Avenue,
into which he had by blind accident strolled—he
thought he would take out and read Winnie
Davies' last letter to him.   It would be a kind
of farewell message from her.   And as he un-
folded these closely-written pages and began, it
seemed to him as if Winnie's voice sounded
strange.   It appeared to be far away.   It appeared to belong to a distant and happy time;

leagues and leagues now lay between him and his sombre surroundings and that cheerful, every-day, hopeful kind of life that Winnie Davies talked about in so simple and blithe a strain.

"Do you know what happened yesterday," she wrote, "when I went down to post a letter? Little Polly Evans had come out from the back shop, and she was sitting on the door-step, and she had a kitten, and she had hold of the kitten by the fore-paws, and was trying to get it to sit up, or to dance, or some nonsense of the kind. But just imagine my astonishment when I over-heard what the little wretch was singing—or trying to sing—I only heard fragments, but I knew what she was after very well: it was im-pudent of the little monkey to make a dance-song of it to please a kitten—but still—but still —and this is what she was trying at:

"'O Llanly bells! O Llanly bells! your sad notes never
    vary;
I hear throughout your trembling chimes the name of
    my lost Mary!
Oh, hush you, bells! oh, hush you, bells! with grief my
    heart is breaking—
Have you no other sound than that—of loving and
    forsaking?'

"'Why, Polly,' says I, 'where did you learn that song?' for I knew she was too small a thing to have heard it at the choir-meetings.

"'My sister Hephzibah sings it at night,' says she, 'when she is ironing the clothes. But they're all singing it.'

"Arthur, my cheeks were burning crimson—I mean my Ordinary Self this time. '*They're all singing it*,' the little monkey said, as innocently as possible. And so, as soon as I had posted father's letter, away I went round by the chapel, and up the hill, for I thought I should like to hear what the Other One—Arthur's Winnie—had to say about this. And when I took the mirror out to find her, you should just have seen her—smirking, and laughing, and as pleased as Punch.

"'Oh,' says I, 'I suppose you're mighty proud just because you've heard that the girls in a Welsh village have taken to singing a particular song?'

"'You mind your own business, Miss Ordinary,' she says, as bold as brass. 'If there are better judges of music than the girls in a Welsh village, I don't know where you will find them.'

"'And I suppose,' says I (for she was looking so happy and stuck-up that it quite annoyed me), 'that you think the popularity of a song in a little corner of Wales means conducting a cantata in St. James' Hall or at the Crystal Palace?'

"But you should have seen how *superior* she was!

"'Miss Ordinary,' she says, 'if you are so very commonplace and unimaginative, let me tell you that small beginnings have sometimes great endings. *They're all singing it:* well, if you see nothing in that—if you do not understand what that means—then I say you are not fit to have made the acquaintance of—you know who I mean; and I will thank you to go away home, and resume your commonplace drudgery, and your narrow views. *I* have faith. *I* can look forward. I don't want to have anything to do with you; I do not wish to associate with you; you can be off now, please!'

"Did you ever hear of such conceit!

"'Oh,' says I, 'perhaps, when the great opera comes to be produced at Covent Garden, you will allow me to pass in to some quiet corner, where I can sit and watch?'"

"'*You!*' she says, with the greatest contempt. 'You would be shaking in your shoes. You would be dreading failure. Whereas *I* have no fear. *I* know.'

"Indeed, dear Arthur, she was just full of confidence and assurance, and too proud almost to speak to, simply because the Llanly girls had taken to singing your song. And I may as well tell you that she was looking none so ill—considering the absence of somebody—and she was wearing, instead of the shell-brooch, the silver anchor, for who was to know who gave it to her——"

Of a sudden he ceased reading this gay and garrulous letter. The mention of his little present to her recalled to him that out at his lodgings there were countless letters and also a number of small trinkets that Winnie Davies had sent him since his coming to London; and how could he go away and leave them behind? These were his secret and sacred treasures: were the detectives to be allowed to overhaul them, to pore over her artless confidences, to guess at hidden meanings known only to himself and her? At any cost of danger these things must be rescued. Even if his lodgings were being watched, might there not be a moment of carelessness? He would be cautious in venturing near; a single second—and a latch-key ready in his fingers—would suffice to get him into the house; as cautiously would he come out again, bringing with him what thereafter could never be profaned. So he debated and debated within himself—fearing and reassuring himself by turns —as the busy world of London woke again; and in the end he was irresistibly drawn away out toward that suburb which hitherto he had avoided with an unnamable dread.

After long delay, and with the greatest circumspection, he ventured to approach his lodgings. It was now past nine, and the omnibuses and tramway-cars had carried the bulk of the business men away into the city; the neighborhood was comparatively quiet. As far as he could make out there was no one keeping observation on the house; so, plucking up courage, he went quickly to the door, opened it, and let himself in, and to his delight found the way clear before him. Hurrying upstairs to his own room, a few seconds enabled him to gain possession of those various little nothings that to him were invaluable; he put them in his breast-pocket, next his heart—they would go with him whither he was going; and now he had but to make good his escape.

At the foot of the stairs he met his landlady— a tall, thin, rather sad-looking woman, in widow's weeds—who seemed frightened.

"Oh, sir, you've come back, sir—and—and a gentleman from the bank, sir, 'e called yesterday evening, and was most p'tickler in his questions, sir, and couldn't understand it——"

"From the bank?" Arthur Hughes repeated, staring at the woman.

"Yes, sir. And another one"—she did not say "gentleman"—"'e came this morning, not 'arf a hour ago, and there was more questions, and what could I say, sir? For you as never was out all night before——"

There was a sharp rat-tat at the door. Arthur Hughes looked alarmed. The landlady stepped along the passage and answered the summons.

"Yes, sir, he's here now," she said to the stranger.

And instinctively the young man knew—and quailed.

"Mr. Arthur Hughes, I believe?" said the new-comer, civilly enough. "My name is Jameson—Inspector Jameson. I have been sent by Cripps' bank to make some inquiries; of course they were very much astonished at your not turning up yesterday afternoon."

"But—but what do you want?" the young man said, with a ghastly pallor on his face.

"Oh, merely that you should come with me to the bank, and give any explanation you see fit. That's all," said the detective, quite coolly. "You have no objection, I presume. We'd better have a hansom; the partners were very much concerned about your not showing up yesterday."

He surrendered himself in a blind sort of fashion. His desperate stratagem—unless there was still some wild chance of escape—had failed. He was in the hands of the law. And his old father? And "sweet Winnie Davies, down by the sea?"

CHAPTER III

A MYSTERY

And the law, as he knew, was inexorable. Unless some unforeseen opportunity might still present itself of his being able to slip away out of the clutches of these people—to disappear, leaving no trace behind him—there would be no mercy shown to him or his. There would be no consideration extended to the white-haired old minister away down there in Wales, nor yet to the young girl whose whole future life would be overshadowed by her former relationship with a felon. The story would get into the papers; there would be a trial; he could do nothing to prove his innocence; and it was the business of the prosecution to believe the worst. Already he seemed to regard himself as a convicted criminal. The inspector seated beside him in the hansom cab was his jailer—it was a wonder he had not produced a pair of handcuffs. And yet this man, no doubt, had his own family ties; most likely, when he went home at night, his children would come clambering on to his knee, convinced that he was the kindest of fathers. It was only when he acted as part of that dread machine, the law, that he became as implacable and inexorable as itself.

For a time, as the hansom carried them rapidly away into the city, the young man was silent and absorbed; and his companion did not seek to intrude upon his dark meditations. But at length Arthur Hughes said, almost wearily:

"I suppose they think I stole the money?"

"Oh! as for that," rejoined the inspector, with an amiable cheerfulness, "there has been no charge brought against you as yet—not at all. It certainly looked awkward your not returning to the bank; and they were naturally very much concerned about it. With a large sum of money like that in your possession, it was possible you might have been robbed or murdered. But of course you will give them all the necessary explanations——"

"I cannot!" the young man exclaimed, in his despair. "How can I explain? I know nothing. When the bag was stolen, I did not see who took it. I had turned for a moment to speak to a stranger, and in the same instant the satchel was snatched away—I suppose by an accomplice of the man who spoke to me. It was all the work of a second. It was as if the satchel had vanished. I ran up and down—searched everywhere——"

He stopped. What was the use of trying to convince this man? It was the business of the law to assume his guilt.

"It would have been better if you had returned to the bank and reported the robbery," observed the inspector, dispassionately.

"I was frightened and bewildered," the young man confessed. "I made sure they would not believe me—the story would sound incredible—and I had nothing to show by way of proof. And I suppose they will not believe me now. You," said he, turning to his companion as if with a challenge, "do you believe that I have not made away with that money? Do you believe that I don't know where a single farthing of it is?"

"Oh, as for that," said the inspector, evasively, "I must remind you again that at present there is no charge against you. You are not even in custody."

"Not in custody!" said Hughes, with a stare.

"No," said the other, coolly. "But if you had refused to come with me to the bank, I should have been forced to give you into custody. It is much better as it is. And I have no doubt you will be able to give a quite satisfactory account of the whole matter when we get to Cripps'."

So he was not yet in custody? And there had been no charge brought against him that would involve his immediate arrest? Was there still some chance, then, of his being allowed to carry his original plan into execution—to make sure that his best and dearest should come to no reproach through him? For he had not revealed his intention to any one; that was his own dark secret; escape and disappearance, and thereafter the silence of unknown waters, might even yet be possible.

But little indeed did Arthur Hughes anticipate what was now about to happen. They had just arrived at Cripps', and were crossing the pavement, when a gentleman came hurriedly out. The moment he cast eyes on young Hughes, an expression of astonishment—coupled with something of relief, too—appeared on his face; and he came forward quickly.

"Good heavens! Hughes, what could you mean by sending me such a letter?" he said, in a serious undertone. "I was just about to drive out to your lodgings, to see what had happened. But here, come into the bank; I must talk this thing over with you in private."

Arthur Hughes followed submissively; this was Mr. Brangwyn, one of the junior partners, who had been of much service to the young man. As they passed through the general room used by the partners, these gentlemen, sitting at their several tables, looked up and scanned with some curiosity (at least so it seemed to Hughes) their absconding clerk; then Mr. Brangwyn entered a smaller apartment, also overlooking the Strand, shut the door, and bade Hughes be seated.

"Well, this is a pretty business!" said he, affecting an injured tone. "You know that it was in a measure due to me that you came to London, and got a place in this bank; then, in conse‑ quence of something connected with the bank, you go and propose to commit suicide; and so, in a measure I am made responsible for the taking away of a fellow-creature's life. Do you call that fair treatment? It seems to me an ill return for what little I have been able to do for you. And suicide! such a cowardly way of escaping from trouble——"

"Mr. Brangwyn," Arthur Hughes gasped out, "I never said a word about suicide!"

"Good gracious, man! what are you talking about!" the junior partner exclaimed, impatiently. "Here is your letter. Here is your letter that I found lying on my table not more than ten minutes ago."

He went to a drawer.

"Yes, I know I sent you a letter," the young man said, quickly. "And—and I confess that I had made up my mind to get on board a ship and slip over the side some dark night; not to escape from anything that might happen to me, but to save my old father—and—and another—from the shame that might come of a prosecution. But

3

no one was to know. It was to be my secret.
And it was not likely I should tell you about it
in a letter."

"Bless my soul, can you read your own handwriting? What do you call that? Read—read
for yourself!"

Arthur Hughes took the letter that was given
to him; and as he regarded it, there was amazement—and even consternation—in his eyes. For
this that he saw before him, line after line, was
not what he had written in that dingy little coffee-house, but what he had been thinking during the time of his writing. Here was the literal
truth. Here were no formal sentences, stu-
diously vague, designed to cover the desperate
scheme he had planned out for himself; but in
place of these the actual thoughts and emotions,
hot and tumultuous, that had surged through his
brain when, as he thought, he was bidding
adieu to life. He read on in breathless bewilderment; for he could not but recognize the
fact that these things had been present to his
mind all the while he was penning that farewell
message. And by what subtle alchemy had the
transformation been effected?

"DEAR MR. BRANGWYN"—this is what he beheld before him, undoubtedly in his own handwriting—"You have been a good friend to me,

and it is with the deepest grief and sorrow in my heart that I say good-by to you, in circumstances that will lead you to suspect me of the basest ingratitude. This afternoon my satchel, containing £7,560 belonging to the bank, was stolen from me at the counter of the London and Westminster, Temple Bar Branch; and as I cannot describe the person who took it, I suppose any one would naturally conclude I myself had made away with the money, and there would be a prosecution. I should not mind that for myself, whatever might happen; but I cannot bear the idea of bringing such shame on my old father, who has lived all his life in respect and honor, and can only have a few years more before him now. And Winnie Davies—the daughter of the schoolmaster at Llanly—I think you will remember her; you said she was the prettiest girl you had seen in Wales; and proud I was that day. She and I were to have been married if things had gone well; but that is all over now; and the only desire I have in my mind is to make sure that no disgrace may fall on my father or on her through me. I am about to take a passage, under an assumed name, in a steamer going to America; and some night I will slip over the side; and no one will guess. My father and Winnie will wonder for a while why I do not write; but my father is an old man; in the natural course he will pass away without suspecting; and Winnie will forget, and marry and be happy. Mr. Brangwyn, I hope you do not think I touched the money. No; I am almost sure you will not think that; but the other partners know little or nothing about me; and they are business men—they would want a strict inquiry; and I have nothing with which to prove my innocence. But that is about myself; and I do not wish to speak about myself; it is all over with me, and my hopes as to music, and with other hopes: what is one human being more or less in the world? It is about those dearest to me that I wish to speak; and I beg this thing from you with a full heart—it is an appeal almost from the grave, and you will not refuse. If my father and Winnie should come to London to make inquiries about me, they will almost certainly go to you, knowing of your goodness to me; and they will ask news of me. Now, dear Mr. Brangwyn, this is my last prayer to you: be kind to them and cheer them. Tell them that I was ambitious—that I went away—that they may expect to hear from me after a while. Do not say anything to them about the money. They are poor; they could not make any restitution to the bank; besides, if they know about the loss, they might couple it with my going away. Be kind to them. The one is an old man who has already come through many troubles and trials; the other is a young girl whose opening life should not be clouded by sad memories. If they come to London, send them away cheerful and hopeful. This is my last prayer to you, and it comes to you as from the other world.

"ARTHUR HUGHES."

"Now," said the banker, in simulated indignation (for in truth he was glad enough to find the young man alive and well, his sinister design frustrated at least for the moment), "perhaps you will say that is not a threat to commit suicide?"

But Arthur Hughes was still staring at the paper, utterly confounded.

"That is not the letter I sent to you!" he said.

"Do you deny that it is in your handwriting? Who is likely to have known of all these private matters but yourself?" were the next questions.

"It is in my handwriting," Hughes said. "And—and what is more—it is the truth. It is what I was thinking all the time. I must have written it—and yet—yet I did not intend writing it; the fact is, Mr. Brangwyn, the letter I did actually send you was quite different from this. I cannot understand it. I was most anxious to hide from every one what I intended doing——"

"And a very pretty scheme it was!" said the young banker. "Why, my good fellow, it is about the maddest piece of Quixotism I ever heard of! To save your friends from a little anxiety and trouble—which is about all that could be involved in an inquiry into the circumstances of the robbery—you propose to deprive an old man of his only son, and a young girl of her sweetheart, to say nothing of throwing away your own life, which you have no right to do. And so I only got to know the truth by some incomprehensible accident? Your hand deceived your eye, or something of that kind? Well, whatever it is, there is to be no more talk about suicide. What you must do now is to come along at once to Scotland Yard——"

Arthur Hughes started and changed color; and the banker instantly noticed that involuntary tremor of apprehension.

"Nothing serious," said he, good-naturedly. "You must give them such particulars of the robbery as you can. A clerk in the London and Westminster remembers something of a man who was standing at the counter just before your satchel was lost."

"I could identify the man who spoke to me anywhere!" young Hughes said with eagerness; for those shackles and trammels that his sensitive imagination had bound upon him seemed to be falling off one by one, and he was beginning to breathe a little more freely.

"And you need not be afraid about yourself, Hughes," the banker continued, "as you appear from your letter to have been. My partners as well as myself accept your story, though you must perceive you did a very foolish thing in not at once returning to the bank yesterday afternoon. And about the money: the larger notes cannot have been negotiated, and the numbers will be in all the papers to-morrow; the damage will not be so great, even if we do not get hold of the men. Now, come along. We will take Inspector Jameson with us—and the less time we lose the better."

And so, after all, Arthur Hughes found himself in that dreaded Scotland Yard. But of what happened to him there—whom he saw—what questions were put to him—or how he answered them, he had but the haziest knowledge. For one thing, he had been up all night, wandering through those dark and silent streets. Then he had had no food since the previous day. But above all, the distressing emotions that had shaken him had left him the mere wreck of his natural self. He had, as it were, tasted the bitterness of death; and now that he had been plucked back from the very verge of the grave, he had not quite recovered his full perceptions.

How had all this come about? By what mysterious means had Mr. Brangwyn become possessed of his secret? Who had betrayed him, when the fulfilment of his scheme of self-sacrifice seemed within his reach?

"Mr. Brangwyn," he said suddenly, when they were on their way back to the bank, "will you show me that letter again?"

The letter was produced, and Hughes studied it long and reflectively.

"No; I never wrote it," he said. "I never wrote that. That is what I had in my mind, certainly; it is true enough; but the letter I sent you was different. Even the ink: the ink I wrote with was violet; this is black."

"The color of ink may change, you know," said Mr. Brangwyn.

"Yes; but not what you have written with it —unless—unless——"

He paused for a second or two in silence. He began to recall the circumstances in which he had become possessed of the violet-hued ink. He recollected his bewilderment and consternation on finding the money gone; his rushing down the narrow thoroughfare; his accidentally knocking over the little Eastern-looking man; his apology; the presentation of the small phial; and his subsequent writing of the letters. And that lilac-colored fluid, the curious odor of which had risen to his nostrils the moment he had opened the bottle: had it some occult and mysterious effect on brain and vision, so that the writer could not see what he was actually writing? Or had it some strange necromantic power of changing, along with its change in color, that which was written into what the writer had really been thinking? And had the Malay, or Lascar, or Hindoo given him this truth-telling ink in order to do him a mischief?

"I suppose I must have written this letter," said he, absently. "No one but myself could have written it. No one but myself knew all the circumstances. And yet I don't remember writing it. No, indeed; what I remember writing was entirely different. I wrote you a merely formal note saying I was about to leave the country, and begging you as a favor not to make inquiries down at—down at Llanly. I wished no one to know what had become of me; I wished no one to suspect——"

"You must have been out of your mind to be contemplating such things!" said the banker, in a kindly way. "But whatever you intended to write, it is a very good thing that the letter I actually received put matters so very plainly; for I mean to see that that delusion about suicide and self-sacrifice is banished out of your head. Romanticism, my dear fellow: it's your Celtic nature, all simmering with high-flown notions; what you want is a little cool, calm common-sense of a wholesome Saxon kind. And the best thing now, after we have reported ourselves at the bank, is for you to go away home to your lodgings, and have some food, and lie down and get some sleep. You look tired; pranks like walking about all night are not good for the nervous system."

And this advice the young man eventually followed, walking home by the Blackfriars Road, in order to have another glance at the coffee-house in which he had written the three letters. He regarded it with a secret dread; he had suffered much in that dusky little place; it was there he had bade good-by to life. And if that extreme step were no longer necessary—if there was to be no public inquiry, no prosecution, that could bring shame on his dear ones at home—so far well; but his own case was not much bettered. For had he not cut himself off from kith and kin; and made an outcast of himself; and bade a last adieu to the girl who, brave in her love, had chosen to throw in her lot with his? He could not go to them now and try to explain away those letters he had sent them. He had signed the decree of his own banishment. He was to live, it was true; but he was to live alone, apart, and silent. It almost seemed to him, while he

walked slowly and listlessly away out to Kennington, as though life in such conditions were
not much preferable to a grave in the wide Atlantic seas.

When he reached his lodgings he was surprised
to find a telegram and a letter awaiting him, and
he was still more startled by the contents of the
former:

"For heaven's sake do nothing rash. Your
father and I are coming to see you at once.

"WINNIE."

What could it mean? His father and Winnie
Davies on their way to London?

Then he quickly turned to the letter, to see if
that would afford any explanation. But as he
read on, it soon became clear to him that these
rambling, whimsical, light-hearted pages had no
connection whatever with recent and tragic
events. This merry epistle belonged to the
happy time—before life had grown black: doubtless she had written and posted it before his farewell message had reached her. And it was with
a strange kind of feeling that he regarded her
in this gay mood.

"Do you know," she wrote, "that there has
been a most desperate fight between me and that
Other Winnie; and if we remain on speaking
terms, that's about all that can be said. This is

how it came about. You remember Dick Griffith? Well, when he came home from Bristol last week he brought for me a most beautifully-bound copy of 'The Songs of Wales,' and he called and left it, with a message. And I confess, Arthur, I was very much pleased; for blue smooth morocco is *so* nice, and only a single line of gold; but somehow—there was a suspicion—I grew uncomfortable—I was frightened of that Other One—and at last I went and opened the mirror.

"'Have you got anything to say?' I asked. (You should have seen her temper!)

"'Send that book back at once!' she cried. 'As politely as you like—but back it goes, and at once! I tell you I will not allow you to accept any present from any young man.'

"Well, Arthur, my Ordinary Self—I told you what a mean, shabby, useless, commonplace kind of creature she is—began to fret and grumble, and that only made the Other Self more indignant.

"' For one thing,' she said, 'if you had an atom of pride, you would refuse to look at any collection of Welsh songs that did not include "The Bells of Llanly," and that had not the name of Arthur Hughes in the index. But you—who are you? a contemptible creature! It's a good thing Arthur knows so little about you!'

"'And you,' I retorted (for I was a little bit angry)—'you give yourself pretty fine airs, all because of your constancy in absence! It is so rare a virtue! It is so wonderful a thing that a girl should keep to her plighted troth!'

"'I do not give myself airs!' she said, with most infinite assurance. 'I take no credit for my constancy at all! And why? Simply because there is no one like him; there is no one to compare with him; and, besides that, I can look forward and see what is awaiting him in the future. But *you—you* don't understand such things; you are a poor wretch. However, I'm going to have one word more with you before I'm done; and I will thank you to listen. You know what Dick Griffith is; he's always dangling after somebody. And you know what that present means. If you keep it, then he will call and see you. Then he will call again. Then he will come in of an evening, to chat with your father. Then he will walk home with you from the meetings of the choir. And then perhaps— some Sunday morning—oh, you despicable, deceitful craven!—you will allow him to go away out to Megan's farm with you—and he will dawdle about, while you pick a few wild flowers to send to London. To send to London! You miserable wretch! But I have warned you! I will keep an eye on you. You can't any longer

pretend ignorance of what presents and visits
may lead to, in the case of a girl whose sweetheart is far away, and who finds herself pretty
much alone. I am going to make you check all
those things at the very outset, my fine madam!'

"'But if Arthur allows me to keep it,' I said,
rather sullenly, 'what right would you have to
interfere then?'

"This made her angrier than ever; you never
saw anything like it!

"'What! you would ask for permission? You
would impose on his generosity? For shame!
Have you no finer feeling at all?'

"'That morocco is as smooth as velvet or silk;
that's what I know.'

"She tried to wither me with scornful glances.

"'No, you have no shame. I must take another way with you. You must be compelled and
coerced. No presents from any young man so
long as I have the mastery over you! I order
you to pack up that book, write a note, and send
them off forthwith. I will undertake that there
shall be no parleyings, no hesitations: I tell you,
you have got to deal with ME!'

"So you see what a remorseless tyrant she is,
dear Arthur; and there was nothing for it but
to cover up again that beautiful blue book, and
send it away. You may say that I earned the
approval of my conscience; but that isn't so, for

I haven't any; it's my Other Self who has the conscience; and she only uses it when she wants to terrify me. Can you wonder that we are hardly on speaking terms? "

And so the careless, playful, prattling letter went on; but he grew less and less interested. It had no bearing on the present circumstances; it had been written in happier moments. But this telegram, with its announcement that his father and Winnie Davies were on their way to London? He stared at the oblong piece of paper —comprehending nothing.

CHAPTER IV

A REUNION

On the afternoon of the following day two strangers, an old man and a young girl, arrived at Paddington Station. They had no luggage save such bits of things as they carried; the porters paid little attention to them; and for a second or two they seemed confused and bewildered by the bustle and echoing din of this vast place. But presently the white-haired old minister and the timid, pretty, shy-eyed girl along with him, had instinctively followed the crowd to the outside platform; and here the minister (with some nervous diffidence) engaged a four-wheeled cab; the man was given an address in Kennington; and then the two travellers resigned themselves to the long and tedious drive toward that distant quarter of the town.

For a time they were silent—silent and pre-occupied; and the faces of both were anxious and careworn. But presently the minister, looking out of the window at those unknown streets and thoroughfares, said in an absent sort of way:

"It is a great city, that has swallowed up the lives and souls of many. Thousands and thousands of poor human creatures have gone down in its deep waters, with hardly even a cry——"

"But not Arthur—not our Arthur!" the girl interposed, piteously. "He could not have been so rash, so desperate; he must have got my telegram; and if he knew we were coming to see him, he would certainly remain in London; surely he would not do anything dreadful if he knew we were on our way to him——"

"And if we are too late," the old man said, with a certain calm and sad resignation, "if the boy has committed this sin, it is not for us to become his judges. The great Judge alone can read the hearts of men: he alone can make allowance for motives: he can forgive much to one that has loved much." Then he murmured to himself: "*Quia multum amavit—quia multum amavit.*"

But she—the girl sitting here, with her pale face harassed and apprehensive, and with those beautiful violet eyes showing that tears had visited them only too frequently during the past anxious hours—was she likely to condemn too harshly? The letter she had received, the letter that conveyed to her the terrible tidings that had brought her thus suddenly to London, had breathed the very spirit of unselfishness. Even now, in this cab, as they traversed the ceaseless thoroughfares of this great desert of a city, she could recall each simple and pathetic phrase and sentence; it was as if he himself were talking to her; and as if the appeal were to her very heart of hearts.

"After all," he had written—or, at least, this was what she had read—"After all, this resolution I have come to is but a poor enough return for the great love and affection that both my father and yourself have given me. Think of the long years of care he has bestowed on me, and constant sympathy and generous consideration; never had any son such a father. But when I come to speak of you, my dearest, my very dearest, what am I to say? Did you ever understand your own courage, your own independence and disinterestedness, when you decided to cast in your lot with mine? Again and

again I have told you I was not worthy of such
loyal and self-sacrificing love; I have shown you
how precarious was my position—how uncertain
my future; but no—you were always the proud
one—you were not to be daunted." . . . "And
now, after having received so much devoted
affection and kindness and sympathy from my
two dear ones, do you think I am going to let
any disgrace fall on them through any doings of
mine? No, no. They are of importance; I am
nothing. Some one else will write the *Caradoc*
cantata—though he may not know of your clever
suggestion that an under-wail of *Morfa Rhuddlan*
should run all through it; and perhaps you will
go to hear it at the Hereford Musical Festival;
and you will say, 'It may be Arthur could have
written it as well as that; but perhaps he could
not; it was merely promise in his case, that had
no chance of fulfilment.' I wish I could have
completed a little song I meant to send you. I
had just about got the air in my head when the
dreadful thing happened, and now all that has
gone by. A darkness has fallen over my life—
such shred of life as now remains to me. And a
deeper darkness is to follow." . . . "My dearest,
how kind to me you were in the old days! Do
you remember the wood beyond Megan's farm;
and the little plank bridge over the brook; and
the Sunday mornings in spring-time when you

used to go to gather anemones, and wild hya-
cinths, and campions? The neighbors used to
say we were only boy and girl; but we were looking far ahead; and you were always the hopeful
one, the light-hearted one, with more than the
courage of a woman. As we sat and talked, I
saw strange things in your eyes—dreams and
pictures—pictures of the long years before us—
and you always by my side—and perhaps one or
two of the things you prophesied come true—and
myself very grateful to you for your constant
faith and upholding and courage. It was a
happy time. You put a kind of fairyland round
the poor assistant clerk at the slate-works; and
love was the light and color of it; and the music
that was in the air was the sound of your voice.
So much, and far more, you did for me: is it
likely I should hesitate when I find before me a
means of saving you—and saving my father—
from having to hang your head in shame?" . . .
"And now, Winnie, this is farewell between you
and me—a farewell forever in this world. When
you get this letter I shall have taken my passage in an outward-bound steamer; but I shall
never reach any port. There will be no arrest
of the absconding clerk; the Atlantic will make
sure of that. And of course you know that I am
innocent—that I did not take the money; others
might be more difficult to convince; but this

step now will guard you from any possible disgrace on my account. And you will forget me
soon; I wish that, for I wish you to be happy.
If I were alive, it would break my heart to think
of your marrying any one else; but the dead
have no hearts to break. And so, good-by forever in this world—good-by, and God bless you
—and do your best to forget all there was between you and me.

"ARTHUR HUGHES."

Would these monotonous and sombre thoroughfares never end? She seemed to have got lost
in a very ocean of streets and houses—an ocean
dull and dismal, vast and shoreless, the unceas-
ing, inarticulate noise of which was stupefying
to the brain. How different from the pleasant woodland ways round Llanly, about which
the poor banished lad must have been thinking when he penned this farewell message!
And had she not been largely instrumental in
severing him from that quiet and simple life and
consigning him to this great and dreadful city?
Was not she in a measure responsible for this
that had happened—though what it was she could
not as yet in any wise conjecture? For it was
all a bewilderment to her—a bewilderment of
dismay, and piteous longing, and trembling hope,
and feverish impatience. She sat silent now;

those sentences from his letter burning clear, as it were, before her eyes. She hardly paid heed to what was outside—to that endless procession of gloomy houses that went by like a dream. And the old man was silent too; it was hardly ι time for talk.

At last, after what had appeared to them an interminable journey, the cabman drew up in front of a house in the Kennington Park Road. The sudden cessation of the noise and rattle was a startling thing; perhaps it was that that caused Winnie Davies' face to blanch as if in fear. But the minister was apparently quite calm and collected. He got out; glanced at the number of the house to see that it was correct; paid the cabman what he asked; and then crossed the pavement, the girl following. He knocked at the door.

The moments of delay that ensued were terrible; the silence was terrible. The house was as a house of the dead. Were they too late, then? Neither spoke. The girl's hands, folded upon the little bag she was carrying, trembled somewhat; but she did not know that. She was watching and listening, with a nervous strain that almost made it impossible for her to breathe.

Then there was a sound; the door opened; a tall, thin, sad-visaged woman appeared.

"Is—is Mr. Arthur Hughes at home?" the

minister asked: there was only the slightest tremor in his voice.

"No, sir," the landlady made answer; and yet, strangely enough, she stepped back a little as if inviting these visitors to pass. "Not yet, sir. But he left a message, sir, that if you and the young lady was to arrive before he came back, I was to say he would be home as soon as he could——"

"He left that message to-day—this morning?" the minister said, quickly, but still maintaining that outward calm.

"Yes, sir," said the melancholy-visaged woman; "and if you would kindly step in and wait a little, sir, which it is near his usual time of coming home in any case——"

"And he is quite well, I presume?" the minister said, with something of hesitation, as he passed into the lobby, followed by the trembling girl.

"Oh, yes, sir—leastways he has been a little flurried and hanxious, as any one could see, the last day or two," answered the landlady, as she showed them upstairs to the young man's room. She was very civil. She offered them tea, which both declined. Indeed, Winnie Davies was hardly capable of responding to the good woman, so entirely was she overcome by this agony of suspense which she had come through. She sat limply in her chair, her hands clinched nervously together; her breathing low and strained. It had been a sore ordeal.

But all at once a new vitality seemed to leap through her frame. She sprang to her feet— listening intently.

"It's Arthur! it's Arthur!" she cried.

She rushed to the door, threw it open, went out on to the landing; and the next moment she had caught her lover by the hand—by both hands—by the arm—and was caressing him, and reproaching him, and pulling him into the room, all at the same time. She was laughing and crying; her face beaming with delight, and yet her dark lashes swimming with tears; and it looked as though she could not let go her hold of him, so eager was she to assure herself that he was alive and well.

"O Arthur, how could you think of doing such a dreadful thing!" she exclaimed—but her upbraiding was only in the words: there was none in her shining and joyful eyes. "To save us from a little trouble, you would go and break our hearts!"

"To say nothing of the grievous sin involved," said the minister, more gravely. "I little thought any son of mine would have contemplated such a crime, no matter what excuse might be blinding his eyes and blunting his conscience."

"But—but—how did you come to know?"
said the young man, in his amazement. "Father—Winnie—what brought you to London?
Who told you what I meant to do? Did Mr.
Brangwyn telegraph to you?"

"Arthur, your own letters!" said Winnie
Davies.

And of a sudden a wild conjecture flashed
through the young man's mind. Had all of
those three farewell letters written in the dingy
little coffee-house been perverted from their
intended purpose? Had each one of them revealed what he was actually thinking at the moment of writing? Had the mysterious ink
betrayed him in each several direction?

And therewithal he sat down and gave them
a minute and circumstantial account of all that
had happened to him during those last eventful
days. And he insisted that in not one of the
three letters he had written had he thrown out
the least hint as to the resolve he had formed;
on the contrary, all three had been composed
with the express object of concealment—to save
his friends from useless sorrow.

"But look, Arthur!" said Winnie Davies, and
with trembling fingers she drew from her pocket
that farewell message that had been haunting
her during all the long journey.

As the young man glanced his eye over these

pages, he seemed to become more and more astounded.

"Yes—yes!" he said. "That is what I was thinking at the time; but not what I wrote to you, Winnie; not what I intended to write, anyway. This is true enough; but I did not want you to know. There could not have been some glamour, some madness, over my eyes, that prevented my seeing what I was actually writing? No, it must have been the ink; the little yellow scoundrel meant to revenge himself on me for having tumbled him into the gutter; and the truth-telling ink was to work mischief——"

"Where is the bottle, Arthur?" Winnie asked promptly.

"I threw it away yesterday morning," he said; and then he added: "I thought I had no further need of it—no, nor of anything else."

"That is a strange phantasy of yours, Arthur," said the minister, slowly, "about the ink that revealed the writer's thoughts in spite of himself —a phantasy it must be, and nothing more. Nevertheless, one might find in it the material for a parable, as to the advantages of telling the truth."

"Oh, I don't care how it all came about!" Winnie Davies cried in her gladness, and now she was standing by the young man's chair, and her arm was on his shoulder, and she had taken

4

his hand in hers. "I don't care at all. If the spiteful little foreigner gave you that ink so that you should get into trouble, he was entirely out-witted; and all that has happened is that your father and I have come to London. And since we are in London, do you know where you must take me? to the Crystal Palace! To-morrow afternoon—Saturday afternoon—to the Crystal Palace!"

"And why the Crystal Palace, Winnie?" he asked.

"Why?" said she, boldly. "Why but that I want to see where you will be standing up in front of the great chorus, conducting the per-formance of your own cantata—if not *Caradoc*, then some other one."

"Dreams!" said he, laughing.

"Dreams come true sometimes," said this un-daunted young person, whose very winsome face and beautiful eyes were all aglow now with pride and happiness and confidence. "And what is more: I am coming to London to be present at that performance—ay, if I have to walk every mile of the way!"

A HALLOWE'EN WRAITH

A HALLOWE'EN WRAITH

I

THE vast bulk of Ben Clebrig was dark in shadow, but the wide waters of Loch Naver shone a soft silver-gray in the moonlight, as Hector MacIntyre, keeper and forester in the far solitudes of Glengorm, came striding along the road toward Inver-Mudal. As he approached the little hamlet—which consists merely of the inn and its surroundings and one or two keepers' cottages—certain small points of red told him of its whereabouts among the black trees; and as he drew still nearer he thought he would let the good people there know of his coming. Hector had brought his pipes with him, for there were to be great doings on this Hallowe'en night; and now, when he had inflated the bag and tuned the drones, there sprang into the profound silence reigning everywhere around the wild skirl of the "Hills of Glenorchy." Surely the sound would reach, and carry its message? If not, here was "Gillie, a Drover," played still more bravely; and again the proud strains of "The Glen's Mine!" By which time he had got near to the inn, and was about to turn down from the highway by the semicircular drive passing the front door.

But here he suddenly encountered a fearful sight. From out of the dusk of the wall surrounding the front garden there came three luminous objects—three globes of a dull saffron hue; and on each of these appeared the features of a face—eyes, mouth, and nose—all flaming in fire. On beholding this terrible thing the tall, brown-bearded forester turned and fled; and the pipes told of his dismay; for they shrieked and groaned and made all sorts of indescribable noises, as if they too were in mortal alarm. Then Mrs. Murray's three children, with victorious shouts of laughter, pursued the tall forester, and kept waving before them the hollowed-out turnips with the bit of candle burning within. When he had got up to the corner of the road, Hector turned and addressed the children, who had come crowding round him, holding up their flaming turnips to cause him still further consternation.

"Well, now," said he, in the Gaelic, "that is a fearful thing to alarm any poor person with. Were you not thinking I should die of fright? And the pipes squealing as well, for they never saw anything like that before. But never mind,

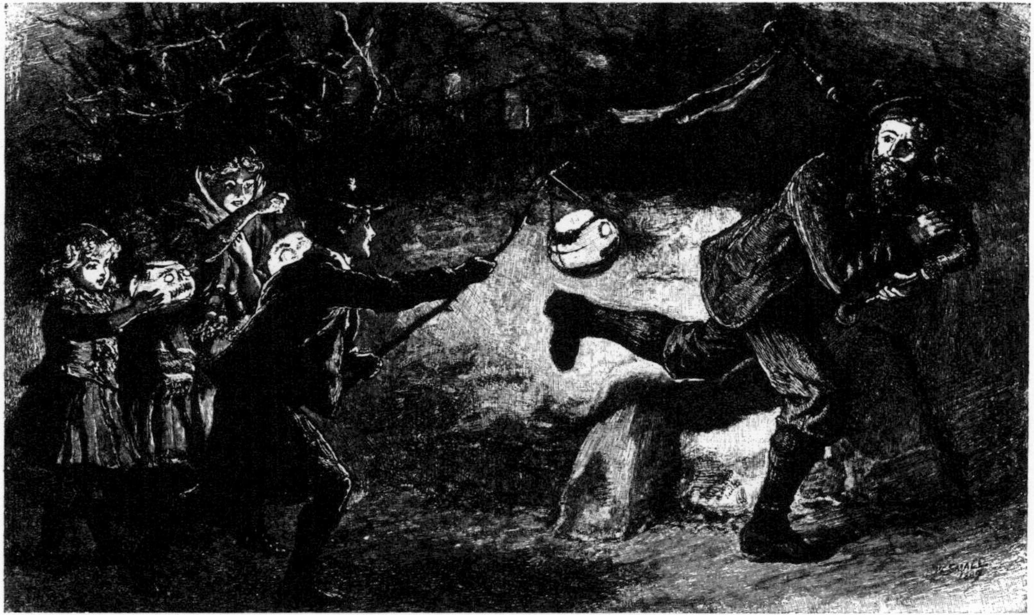

"FROM OUT OF THE DUSK OF THE WALL"

we are going down to the house now; and, do you know, Ronald, and Isabel, and you, little Shena—do you know, I have brought you some of the fir tops that grow in Glengorm. For it is a wonderful place, Glengorm; and the fir tops that grow on the larches there are not as the fir tops that grow anywhere else. They are very small, and they are round, and some are pink, and some are blue, and some are black and white, and some others—why, they have an almond inside them! Oh, it is a wonderful place, Glengorm! but it is not always you can get the fir tops from the larches; it is only on some great occasion like the Hallowe'en night; and let me see, now, if I put any of them in my pocket. Here, Ronald, take the pipes from me, and hold them properly on your shoulder—for one day you will be playing 'Miss Ramsay's Strathspey' as well as any one—and I will search my pockets, and see if I put any of those wonderful fir tops into them."

The children knew very well what all this preamble meant; but neither they nor their elders could have told how it was that Hector Mac-Intyre, every time he came to Inver-Mudal, brought with him packages of sweetmeats, though he lived in one of the most inaccessible districts in Sutherland, Glengorm being about two-and-twenty miles away from anywhere.

However, here were the precious little parcels; and when they had been distributed, Hector took his pipes again, and, escorted by his small friends, went down to the inn.

Well, Mr. Murray, the innkeeper, had also heard the distant skirl of the pipes, and here he was at the door.

"How are you, Hector?" he asked, in the Gaelic. "And what is your news?"

"There is not much news in Glengorm," was the answer.

"And when is your wedding to be?" Mr. Murray said. "We will make a grand day of that day, Hector. And I have been thinking I will get some of the lads to kindle a bonfire on the top of Ben Clebrig—a fire that they will see down in Ross-shire. And there's many a pistol and many a gun will make a crack when you drive up to this door and bring your bride in. For I am one who believes in the old customs; and whether it is a wedding, or the New Year, or Hallowe'en night, I am for the old ways, and the Free Church ministers can say what they like. Now come away in, Hector, my lad, and take a dram after your long walk; there is plenty of hard work before you this evening; for Johnnie has broken his fiddle; and the lasses have not been asked to stand up to a reel for many a day." And then he paused, and said: "And how is Flora Campbell, Hector? Have you any news of her?"

"No," said the forester, in something of an undertone, and his face looked troubled. "I have had no letter for a while back; and I do not know what it means. Her sister that lives in Greenock was taken ill; and Flora said she must go down from Oban to see her; and that is the last I have heard. If I knew her sister's address in Greenock, I would write and ask Flora why there was no letter for so long; but if you send a letter to one called Mary Campbell in such a big place as Greenock, what use is it?"

"But no news is good news, Hector," said Mr. Murray, cheerfully. And therewith he led the way through a stone corridor into the great kitchen, where a considerable assemblage of lads and lasses were already engaged in noisy merriment and pastime.

The arrival of the tall forester and his pipes was hailed with general satisfaction; but there was no call as yet for the inspiriting music; in fact, this big kitchen was given over to the games of the children and the younger boys and girls, a barn having been prepared for supper, and for the celebration of occult Hallowe'en rites when the time came for their elders to take part in the festivities. At present there was a large tub filled with water placed in the middle of the

4*

floor; and there were apples in it; and the youngsters, with their hands behind their backs, were trying to snatch out an apple with their teeth. There was many a sousing of heads, of course—an excellent trial of temper; while sometimes a bolder wight than usual would pursue his prize to the bottom, and try to fasten upon it there; or some shy young damsel would cunningly shove the apple over to the side of the tub, and succeed by mother-wit where masculine courage had failed. Then from the roof, suspended by a cord, hung a horizontal piece of wood, at one end of which was an apple, at the other a lighted tallow candle; and when the cord had been twisted up and then set free again, causing the transverse piece of wood to whirl round, the competitor was invited to snatch with his mouth at the apple, failing to do which secured him a rap on the cheek from the guttering candle. There were all sorts of similar diversions going forward (the origin and symbolism of them little dreamt of by these light-hearted lads and lasses) when little Isabel Murray came up to the big, handsome, good-natured-looking forester from Glengorm.

"Will you burn a nut with me, Hector?" she said, kindly.

"Indeed I will, Isabel, if you will take me for your sweetheart," said he, in reply; "and now

" I WILL SEARCH MY POCKETS "

we will go to the fire, and see whether we are to
be at peace and friendship all our lives."

They went to the hearth; they put the two
nuts among the blazing peats; and awaited the
response of the oracle. Could any augury have
been more auspicious? The two nuts lay together, burning steadily and quickly—a soft love-
flame—no angry sputtering, no sudden explosion
and separation.

"Now do you see that, lamb of my heart?"
said the tall forester, using a familiar Gaelic
phrase.

And no doubt the little lass was very highly
pleased. However, at this moment up came
Mrs. Murray with the announcement that the
children might continue at their games some
time longer, but that the grown-up folk were
wanted in the barn, where supper was awaiting
them.

It was a joyous scene. The huge peat fire
was blazing brightly; the improvised chandelier
was studded with candles; there were a couple
of lamps on the long table, which was otherwise
most sumptuously furnished. And when Hector
MacIntyre, in his capacity of piper, had played
the people in to the stirring strains of "The
Marchioncss of Tweeddale's Delight," he put the
pipes aside, and went and took the seat that had
been reserved for him by the side of the fair-

haired Nelly, who was very smartly dressed for this great occasion, as befitted the reigning beauty of the neighborhood.

"You'll be sorry that Flora is not here to-night," said the fair-haired damsel, rather saucily, to her brown-bearded companion; "and no one to take her place. I suppose there was no one in Sutherland good enough for you, Hector, that you must take up with a lass from Islay. And there is little need for you to dip your sleeve in the burn and hang it up to dry when you go to bed, so that the fire may show you your sweetheart, for well you know already who that is. Well, well, you will have no heart for the merrymaking to-night; for a lad that has his sweetheart away in the south has no heart for anything."

"You'll just mind this, Nelly," said the forester, "not to carry your merrymaking too far this night. Alastair Ross," he continued, glancing down the table toward a huge, rough, red-bearded drover who was seated there, "is not the man to be made a fool of; and if that young fellow Semple does not take heed, he will find himself gripped by the waist some fine dark evening and flung into Loch Naver."

"Oh, you are like all the rest, Hector!" said the coquettish Nelly, with some impatience. "Every one of you is jealous of Johnnie Semple, because he is neatly dressed and has good manners and is civil spoken——"

"What is he doing here at all?" said Hector, with a frown. "Is it a fine thing to see a young man idling about a place with his hands in his pockets just because his uncle is the landlord? If he has learned his fine manners in the towns, why does he not earn his living in the towns? He is no use here."

"Oh, no," said Nelly, with a toss of her head; "perhaps he is not much use on the hill; perhaps he could not set traps and shoot hawks. But he knows all the new songs from the theatres, and he can dance more steps than any one in Sutherland."

"Well, this is what I am telling you, Nelly," her companion said, with some firmness. "I do not know what there is between you and Alastair Ross. If there is anything, as people say, then do not make him an angry man. Let Semple alone. An honest lass should beware of a town dandy like that."

Here this private little conversation was interrupted by Mr. Murray, who rose at the head of the table and called upon the company to fill their glasses. He wished to drink with them, and they did not seem loth. When Hector and his pretty companion found opportunity to resume their talk, he discovered that Nelly was in quite a different mood.

"Well, now, it is a good thing, Hector, that every one knows that you and Flora are to be married; for I can talk to you without Alastair getting red in the face with rage. And when we go out to pull the cabbage-stalks, will you go with me? I know the way into the garden better than you; and we can both go blindfold if you will take my hand."

"But what need is there for you to pull a cabbage-stalk, lass?" said he. "Do you not know already what like your husband is to be?"

Again the pretty Nelly tossed her head. "Who can tell what is to happen in the world?"

"And maybe you would rather not pull a stalk that was tall and straight and strong—that would mean Alastair?" said her companion, glancing at her suspiciously. "Maybe you would rather find you had got hold of a withered old stump with a lot of earth at the root—a decrepit old man with plenty of money in the bank? Or maybe you are wishing for one that is slim and supple and not so tall—for one that might mean Johnnie Semple?"

"I am wishing to know who the man is to be, and that is all," said Nelly, with some affectation of being offended. "And what harm can there be in doing what every one else is doing?"

However, not all Nelly's blandishments and petulant coquetries could induce Hector Mac-

Intyre to take part in this appeal to the divi-
nation of the kale-yard; for when, after supper,
the lads and lasses went away blindfold to pull
the "custock" that was to reveal to them the figure and circumstances of their future spouse, the
big forester remained to have a quiet smoke
with the married keepers and shepherds, who
had no interest in such matters. It was noticed
that he was unusually grave—he who was ordinarily one of the lightest of the light-hearted.
Naturally they put it down to the fact that among
all the merrymaking and sweethearting and spy-
ing into the future of the younger people he
alone had no companion, or rather not the companion whom he would have wished to have;
for Flora, the young girl whom he was to marry,
had left Inver-Mudal for the south in the preceding autumn. And when they had asked if Flora
was quite well, and when he had answered "Oh,
yes," there was nothing further to be said.

II

Now on All-Hallows Eve there is one form of
incantation which is known to be extremely, nay,
terribly potent, when all others have failed. You

go out by yourself, taking a handful of hemp-seed with you. You get to a secluded place, and begin to scatter the seed as you walk along the road. You say, " Hemp-seed, I sow thee; hemp-seed I sow thee; he who is to be my true love, appear now and show thee." And if you look furtively over your shoulder you will behold the desired apparition following you.

When Nelly came back from consulting the oracle of the kale-yard, it appeared that she had received what oracles generally vouchsafe—a doubtful answer.

"What kind of custock did you pull, Nelly? " Hector asked of her.

"Well," said she, "it is not much one way or the other. No, I cannot tell anything by it. But I am going out now to sow the hemp-seed, Hector; and I know I shall be terribly fright-ened—I shall be far too frightened to look over my shoulder; and this is what I want you to do for me: you will stop at the door of the inn and hide yourself; and I will go up the road and sow the hemp-seed; and if anything appears, you will see it. Will you do that, Hector? It is a clear night; you will be sure to see it if there is any-thing."

He did not seem to be in the mood for taking part in these superstitious observances; but he was good-natured, and eventually followed her

to the door. The little walled garden in front of
the Inver-Mudal inn is shaped like a horseshoe,
the two ends of the semicircle touching the main
highway at some distance apart. He saw Nelly
go up toward the main road, and looked after
her absently and without interest. Nay, he was
so little thinking of his promised watch that, as
she was some time over the sowing of the hemp-
seed, he left the shadow of the inn door, and
strolled away up to the main road by the other
fork of the semicircular drive. It was a beautiful clear moonlight night; his thoughts were far
away from these Hallowe'en diversions; he was
recalling other evenings long ago, when Clebrig, as now, seemed joining earth and heaven,
and when there was no sound but the murmuring of the burns through the trackless heather.
The highway up there was white before him; on
the other side was a plantation of young firs,
black as jet. Not even the cry of a startled bird
broke this perfect stillness; the wide world of
mountain and loch and moor was plunged in
sleep profound.

All at once his pipe, that he happened to be
holding in his hand, dropped to his feet. There
before him in the white highway, and between
him and the black belt of firs, stood Flora
Campbell, regarding him with eyes that said
nothing, but only stared in a somewhat sad way,

as it seemed. He was not paralyzed with terror at all. He had no time to ask himself what she was doing there, or how she had come there. Flora Campbell standing there in the road, and looking at him in silence. But the horror came when suddenly he saw that the white highway was empty. He began to shake and shiver as if with extremity of cold. He did not move; he could not move. He knew what had happened to him now. Flora Campbell's wraith had appeared to him. And with what message? The steady gaze of her eyes had told him nothing. If they were anything, they were mournful. Perhaps it was a token of farewell; perhaps it was an intimation of her death. Hardly knowing what he did, and trembling in every limb, he advanced a step or two, so that he could command the whole length of the highway. There was no sign of any living thing there. He could not recall how it was she first appeared; he could not tell in what manner she had gone away; he only knew that a few moments before Flora had been regarding him with steady, plaintive eyes, and that now he was alone with this moonlit road and the black plantation, and Clebrig rising far into the silent heavens.

Then there arose in his heart a wild resolve that, whatever this thing might portend, he must instantly make away for the south, to seek

out Flora Campbell herself. She had something
to say to him, surely, though those mournful
eyes conveyed no intelligible message. Nay, if
she were dead, if this were but a mute farewell,
must he not know? Dazed, bewildered, filled
with terrible misgivings of he knew not what,
he slowly went back to the inn. He had some
vague instinct that he must ask Mr. Murray for
the loan of a stick if he were to set out now to
cross the leagues of wild and mountainous country that lie between Inver-Mudal and the sea.
Mr. Murray, as it chanced, was at the door.

"God's sake, Hector, what is the matter with
you?" he exclaimed, in alarm, for there was a
strange look in the man's face.

"I have seen something this night," was the
answer, spoken slowly and in an undertone.

"Nonsense! nonsense!" the innkeeper said.
"The heads of the young people are filled with
foolishness on Hallowe'en, as every one knows;
but you—you are not to be frightened by their
stories."

"It has naught to do with Hallowe'en," said
Hector, still with his eyes fixed on the ground,
as if seeking to recall something. "Do you
know what I have seen this night? I have seen
the wraith of Flora Campbell—ay, as clear as
daylight."

"I will not believe it, Hector," said Mr. Murray. "You have been hearing all those stories of the witches and fairies on Hallowe'en until your own head has been turned. Why, where did you see the wraith?"

"Up there in the road, and as clear as daylight, for that is the truth. It was Flora herself," the tall forester made answer, not argumentatively, but as merely stating a fact that he knew.

"And did she come forward to you, or did she go away from you?" Mr. Murray asked, curiously.

"I—I am not sure," Hector said, after a little hesitation. "No, I could not say. Perhaps I was not thinking of her. But all at once I saw her between me and the plantation, in the middle of the road; and for a moment I was not frightened; I thought it was Flora herself; then she was gone."

"For you know what they say, Hector," Mr. Murray continued. "When a wraith appears, it is to tell you of a great danger; and if it comes forward to you, then the danger is over; but if it goes away from you, the person is dead."

"Ay, ay; I have heard that too," Hector murmured, as if in sombre reverie. Then he looked up, and said: "I am going away to the south."

"Well, now, that is unfortunate, Hector," the good-natured innkeeper said to him. "For to-

morrow the mail comes north, and you will have
to wait till the next day for the mail going
south, to take you in to Lairg to catch the
train."

"I will not wait for the mail," answered the
forester, who, indeed, knew little about travelling by railway. "To-morrow is Wednesday:
it is the day the big steamer starts from Loch
Inver; perhaps I may be in time."

"Loch Inver!" the other exclaimed. "And
how are you going to get to Loch Inver from
here, Hector?"

"Across the forest," was the simple reply.

"Across the Reay Forest and down by Loch
Assynt? That will be a fearful journey through
the night!"

"I cannot rest here," Hector said. "You will
make some excuse for me to the lads and lasses.
I will leave my pipes; Long Murdoch will do
very well with them. And I will thank you to
lend me a stick, Mr. Murray, for it will be a
rough walk before I have done."

Mr. Murray did more than that; he got his
wife to make up a little packet of food, to which
he added a flask of whiskey; and these he took
out to the young man, along with a shepherd's
staff of stout hazel.

"Good-by, Hector!" said he. "I hope you
will find all well in the south."

"I do not know about that," the forester answered, in an absent sort of fashion; "but I must go and see. There will be no peace of mind for me—there would not be one moment's peace for me—otherwise. For who knows what Flora wanted to say to me?"

III

IT was an arduous task he had set before him; for nine men out of ten it would have been an impossible one; but this young forester's limbs knew not what fatigue was; and in his heart there burned a longing that could not be assuaged. Nor in ordinary circumstances would the loneliness of this night's journey have mattered to him; but his nerves had been unstrung by the strange thing that had happened; and now, as he followed a shepherd's track that led away into the higher moorlands south of the Mudal River, he was conscious of some mysterious influence surrounding him that was of far more immediate concern than the mere number of miles—some forty or fifty—he had to accomplish before noon of the next day. These vast solitudes into which he was penetrating were ap-

parently quite voiceless and lifeless; and yet he
felt as if they knew of his presence, and were
regarding him. A white stone on a dark heather-
covered knoll would suddenly look like a human
face; or again, he would be startled by the moonlight shining on a small tarn set among the black
peat hags. There was no moaning of wind; but
there was a distant murmuring of water; the rills
were whispering to each other in the silence.
As for the mountains—those lone sentinels, Ben
Loyal and Ben Hope and Ben Hee—they also
appeared to be looking down upon the desolate
plain; but he did not heed them, they were too
far away; it was the objects near him that seemed
to know he was here, and to take sudden shapes
as he went by.

Soon he was without even a shepherd's track
to guide him; but he knew the lay of the land;
and he held on in a line that would avoid the
lochs, the deeper burns, and the steep heights
of Meall-an-amair. The moonlight was a great
help; indeed, at this period of his long through-
the-night tramp he was chiefly engaged in trying
to recall how it was he first became sensible that
Flora Campbell's wraith appeared before him.
He saw again—surely he would never forget to
his dying day the most insignificant feature of
the scene—the stone wall of the garden, the
white road, the wire fence on the other side, and

the black plantation of spruce and pine. What had he been thinking about? Not about Nelly; she was some distance in another direction, busy with her charms and incantations. No; he could not tell. The sudden apparition had startled him out of all memory. But what he was most anxious to convince himself was that the phantom had come toward him, rather than gone away from him, ere it disappeared, Mr. Murray's words had sunk deep, though he himself had been aware of the familiar superstition. But now all his endeavors to summon up an accurate recollection of what had taken place were of no avail. He knew not how he first became conscious that the wraith was there—Flora Campbell herself, as it seemed to him—nor how it was he suddenly found himself alone again. He had been terrified out of his senses; he had no power of observation left. This phantasm that looked so like a human being, that regarded him with pathetic eyes, that had some mysterious message to communicate, and yet was silent, had vanished as it had appeared, he could not tell how.

The hours went by; the moon was sinking toward the western hills. And still he toiled on through this pathless waste, sometimes getting into treacherous swamps, again having to ford burns swollen by the recent rains. He was soaked through to the waist; but little he heeded that; his thoughts were of the steamer that was to leave Loch Inver the next day. With the moon going down, darkness was slowly resuming her reign, and it became more difficult to make out the landmarks; but, at all events, the heavens remained clear, and he had the guidance of the stars. And still steadily and patiently and manfully he held on, getting without much serious trouble across the streams that feed Loch Fhiodaig, until eventually he struck the highway running northward from Loch Shin, and knew that so far, at least, he was in the right direction.

Leaving the Corrykinloch road again, he had once more to plunge into the trackless wilderness of rock and swamp and moorland; and the further he went through the black night the less familiar was he with the country. But he had a general knowledge; and what mattered half a dozen miles one way or the other, if only the dawn would show him Ben More on his left, and away before him the silver-gray waters of Loch Assynt? He was less conscious now of the sinister influences of these lonely solitudes; his nervous apprehensions had to give way before his dogged resolve to get out to the western shore in time to catch the steamer; all his attention was given to determining his course by the vague outlines of the higher hills. A wind had arisen, a cold, raw wind it was; but he cared

nothing for that, unless, indeed, it should bring
a smurr of rain and obliterate the landmarks altogether. How anxiously he prayed for the
dawn! If this wind were to bring driving mists
of rain, blotting out both earth and heaven, and
limiting his vision to the space of moorland immediately surrounding him, where would be his
guidance then? He could not grope his way
along the slopes that lie beneath Loch nan Scarir,
nor yet across the streams that fall into Loch
Fionn. So all the more resolutely he held on
while as yet he could make out something of the
land, dark against the tremulous stars.

Again and again he turned his head and
scanned the east, with a curious mingling of impatience and hope and longing; and at length, to
his unspeakable joy, he was able to convince himself that the horizon there was giving faint signs
of the coming dawn. He went forward with a
new confidence, with a lighter step. The horror
of these awful solitudes would disappear with the
declaring day; surely, surely, when the world had
grown white again, he would behold before him,
not this terrible black loneliness of mountain
and mere, but the pleasant abodes of men, and
trees, and the western ocean, and the red-funnelled steamer with its welcome smoke. The
gray light in the east increased. He began to
make out the features of the ground near him;

he could tell a patch of heather from a deep
hole; and could choose his way. The world
seemed to broaden out. Everything, it is true,
was as yet wan and spectral and ill-defined; but
the silence was no longer awful; he had no further fear of the mists coming along to isolate
him in the dark. By slow degrees, under the
widening light of the sky, the various features
of this wild country began to take more definite
shape. Down there in the south lay the mighty
mass of Ben More. On his right rose the sterile
altitudes of Ben Uidhe. And at last, and quite
suddenly, he came in view of the ruffled silvery
surface of Loch Assynt, and the cottages of Inch-
nadamph, and the gray ruins of Ardvreck Castle
on the promontory jutting out into the lake. The
worst of the sore fight with solitude and the night
was over. He gained the road, and his long
swinging stride now stood him in good stead.
Loch Assynt was soon left behind. He followed
the windings of the river Inver. Finally he
came in sight of the scattered little hamlet facing the western seas, with its bridge and its
church and its pleasant woods and slopes, looking all so cheerful and home-like; and there also
was the red-funnelled *Clansman* that was to carry
him away to the south.

IV

THAT long and difficult struggle to get out to
the western coast in time had so far demanded
all his energy and attention; but now, in en-
forced idleness, as the heavy steamer ploughed
her way across the blue waters of the Minch, his
mind could go back upon what had happened
the preceding night, and could also look forward with all sorts of dark, indefinite forebod-
ings.   He began to recall his first association
with Flora Campbell, when she came to Auchnaver Lodge to help the old housekeeper there.
He remembered how neat and trim she looked
when she walked into Strathie Free Church
of a Sunday morning; and how shy she was
when he got to know her well enough to talk a
little with her when they met, in their native
tongue.   Their courtship and engagement had
the entire approval of Flora's master and mistress; for the old housekeeper at the lodge was
now past work; and they proposed to install Hector's wife in her place, and give her a permanent
situation.   The wedding was to be in February
or March; in April the young wife was to move
into the lodge, to get it ready for the gentlemen
coming up for the salmon-fishing.   When the

fishing and shooting of the year were over, Flora
could return to her husband's cottage, and merely
look in at the lodge from time to time to light a
fire or two and keep the place aired. Meanwhile, for this present winter, she had taken a
situation in Oban (she was a West Highland
girl), and had remained there until summoned
away to Greenock by the serious illness of her
sister. Such was the situation; but who could
tell now what was to become of all those fair
prospects and plans? Was it to bid a last farewell to them and to him that the young Highland
girl had appeared—saying good-by with such
mournful eyes? The small parlor in his cottage
—was she never to see the little adornments he
had placed there, all for her sake? Well, then,
if what he feared had come true, no other woman should enter and take possession. There
were dreams of Canada, of Cape Colony, of Aus-
tralia in his brain as he sat there with bent brow
and heavy heart, taking hardly any heed of the
new shores they were now nearing.

This anguish of brooding became at length insupportable; in despair he went to the stevedore,
and said he would be glad to lend a hand with
the cargo as soon as the steamer was alongside
the quay in Stornoway Harbor. And right hard
he worked, too, hour after hour, feeding the
steam crane that was swinging crates and boxes

over and down into the hold.   The time passed more easily in this fashion.   His chum was a good-natured young fellow who seemed rather proud of his voice; at times he sang snatches of Gaelic songs—"Máiri bhinn mheall shuileach" (Mary of the bewitching eyes), or "C'aite 'n caidil an ribhinn?" (Where sleepest thou, dear maiden?).   They were familiar songs; but there was one still more familiar that woke strange echoes in his heart; for Flora Campbell was a west-country girl, and of course her favorite was the well-known "Fear a bhata:"

" I climb the mountains and scan the ocean
For thee, my boatman, with fond devotion,
When shall I see thee?—to-day?—to-morrow?
Oh, do not leave me in lonely sorrow!
    O my boatman, *na horo ailya,*
    O my boatman, *na horo ailya,*
    O my boatman, *na horo ailya,*
A   hundred   farewells   to   you, wherever you   may   be
    going."

That is how it begins in the English; but it was the Gaelic phrases that haunted his brain, and brought him remembrance of Flora's crooning voice, and of a certain autumn evening when he and she and some others went all the way down Loch Naver to Inver-Mudal, Flora and he sitting together in the stern of the boat, and all of them singing the "Fear a bhata."

" FLORA AND HE SITTING TOGETHER IN THE STERN OF THE BOAT, AND ALL OF THEM SINGING THE ' FEAR A BHATA ' "

The *Clansman* left Stornoway that same night, groaning and thundering through the darkness on her way to Skye. Hector did not go below into the fore-cabin. He remained on deck, watching the solitary ray of some distant lighthouse, or perhaps turning his gaze upon the great throbbing vault overhead where Cassiopeia sat, throned upon her silver chair. More than once an aërolite shot swiftly across the clear heavens, leaving a faint radiance for a second or so in its wake; but he took no heed of these portents now. In other circumstances they might mean something; but now a more direct summons had come to him from the unknown world; the message had been delivered, though he had been unable to understand it; and he knew that what was to happen had now happened in that far town of Greenock. And as the slow hours went by, his impatience and longing increased almost to despair. The dark loom of land in the south appeared to come no nearer. The monotonous throbbing of the screw seemed as if it were to go on forever. And as yet there was no sign of the dawn.

But the new day, which promised to be quite insupportable in its tedium and in its fears, in reality brought him some distraction, and that was welcome enough. At Portree there came on board a middle-aged man of rather mean aspect, with broken nose, long upper lip, and curiously set small gray eyes. He carried a big bag which apparently held all his belongings, and that he threw on to the luggage on the forward deck.

"Where's this going to?" called the stevedore.

"Sure 'tis bound for the same place as mesilf," said the new-comer, facetiously; "and that's Philadelphia, begob!"

"We don't call there," retorted the stevedore, dryly; "and you'd better stick to your bundle if you want to see it at Greenock."

And very soon it became apparent that the advent of this excited and voluble Irishman had brought new life into the steerage portion of the ship. He had a glass or two of whiskey. He talked to everybody within hearing about himself, his plans, his former experiences of the United States; and when gravelled for lack of matter, he would fall back on one invariable refrain: "Aw, begob! the Americans are the bhoys!" And in especial were his confidences bestowed on Hector MacIntyre, the shy and reserved Highlander listening passively and without protest to Paddy's wild asseverations.

"Aw, the Americans are the divils, and no mistake!" he exclaimed. "But let me tell you this, sorr, that there's one that's cliverer than them, and that's the Irish bhoy, begob! Sure they talk about the German vote—aw, bather-shin! 'Tis the Irish vote, sorr, that's the mas-ther; and we've got the newspapers. And where would the Republicans or the Dimocrats be widout us?—tell me that av ye plaze! In this —— ould counthry the Irishman is a slave; in Americay he's the masther; and every mother's son of them knows it! Aw, begob, sorr, that's the place for a man! This —— ould counthry isn't fit for a pig to live in! Americay's the place; you may bet your life on it, sorr!"

And suddenly it occurred to Hector that he might gain some information, even from this blathering fool. His thoughts had been running much on emigration during those lonely hours he had passed. If what he dreaded had really taken place, he would return no more to the lone moorlands and hills and lakes of Sutherlandshire. He would put the wide Atlantic between himself and certain memories. For him it would be "Soraidh slàn le tir mo ghràidh"—a long fare-well to Fiunary!

But at present the Irishman would not be questioned; the outflowing of his eloquence was not to be stopped. He was now dealing with the various classes and the various institutions of Great Britain, on each of which he bestowed the same epithet—that of "bloody." The Govern-ment, the newspaper editors, the House of Lords,

5*

the House of Commons, the clergy, the judges, the employers of labor, all were of the same ensanguined hue; and all were equally doomed to perdition, as soon as Ireland had taken up her proper and inevitable position in America. Moreover, the tall and silent Highlander, as he sat and gazed upon this frothing creature as if he were some strange phenomenon, some incomprehensible freak of nature, could not but see that the man was perfectly in earnest.

"Look what they did to John Mitchel! Look at that, now! John Mitchel!"

Hector had, unfortunately, never heard of John Mitchel, so he could not say anything.

"Dying by the road-side!—John Mitchel—to be left to die by the road-side! Think of that, now! What d'ye say to that, now? John Mitchel being left to die by the road-side!"

There were sudden tears in the deep-sunken gray eyes; and the Irishman made no concealment as he wiped them away with his red cotton handkerchief.

"Well, I'm very sorry," Hector MacIntyre replied, in answer to this appeal, "whoever he was. But what could they have done for the poor man?"

"They could have given him a place," the other retorted, with a sudden blaze of anger. "All that John Mitchel wanted was a place. But the " (ensanguined) "Government, would they do it? No, sorr! They let him die by the road-side!—John Mitchel—to die by the road-side!"

"Well, I am thinking," said the forester slowly (as was his way when he had to talk in English), "that if the Government wass to give places to ahl them that would like a place, why, the whole country would be in the public service, and there would be no one left to till the land. And do they give you a place when you go to America?"

"Aw, begob, sorr," said the Irishman, with a shrewd twinkle in his eye, "we get our share!"

Hector could not make out whether his new acquaintance had been to Portree to say good-by to some friends before he crossed the Atlantic, or whether he had been engaged in the crofter agitation which was then attracting attention in Skye. On this latter subject Paddy discoursed with a vehement volubility and a gay and audacious ignorance; but here Hector was on his own ground, and had to interfere.

"I am thinking you will not be knowing much about it," he observed, with a calm frankness. "The great Highland clearances, they were not made for deer at ahl, they were not made for sportsmen at ahl, they were made for sheep, as many a landlord knows to his cost this day, when he has the sheep farms on his lands and cannot get them let. And the deer forests, they are the worst land in a country where the best land is poor; and if they were to be cut up into crofts to-morrow, there is not one crofter in twenty would be able to earn his living, even if he was to get the croft for no rent at ahl. Oh, yes, I am as sorry as any one for the poor people when they increase in their families on such poor land; but what would be the use of giving them more peat hags and rocks? Can a man live where neither deer nor sheep nor black cattle can live; and even the deer come down in the winter and go wandering for miles in search of a blade of bent-grass? "

However, the Irishman would not accept these representations in any wise. He suspected this grave, brown-bearded Highlander of being an accomplice and hireling of the (ensanguined) landlords; and he might have gone on to denounce him, or even to provoke an appeal to fisticuffs (which would have been manifestly imprudent) had it not suddenly occurred to him that they might go down below and have a glass of whiskey together. Hector saw him disappear into the fore-cabin by himself, and was perhaps glad to be left alone.

Steadily the great steamer clove her way onward, by the islands of Raasay and Scalpa, through the narrows of Kyle Akin and Kyle Rhea, past the light-house and opening into Isle

Ornsay, and down toward the wooded shores of
Armadale. The day was fair and still; the sea
was of an almost summer-like blue, with long
swathes of silver calm; the sun shone on the
lower green slopes that seemed so strangely
voiceless, and on the higher peaks and shoulders
of the hills, where every corrie and watercourse
was a thread of azure among the ethereal rose-
grays of the far-reaching summits. Even the
wild Ardnamurchan ("The Headland of the
Great Waves") had not a flake of cloud clinging
to its beetled cliffs; and the long smooth roll
that came in from the outer ocean was almost
imperceptible. Toward evening the *Clansman*
sailed into Oban Bay. The world seemed all on
fire, so far as sea and sky were concerned; but
Kerrera lay in shadow, a cold and livid green;
while between the crimson water and the crimson
heavens stood the distant mountains of Mull;
and they had grown to be of a pale, clear, trans-
parent rose-purple, so that they seemed a mere
film thinner than any isinglass.

V

THERE was abundance of time for him to go
ashore and make inquiries; but nothing had been
heard of Flora Campbell since she had left.
However, he managed to get the Greenock address of her sister, Mary Campbell, and with
that in his possession he returned on board.
Thereafter the monotonous voyage was resumed
—away down by the long peninsula of Cantyre
and round the Mull, up again through the estuary
of the Clyde, until, at four o'clock on Friday
afternoon, the *Clansman* drew in to Greenock
quay; and Hector MacIntyre knew that within
a few minutes he would learn what fate had in
store for him, for good or irretrievable ill.

He found his way to the address that had been
given him—a temperance hotel at which Mary
Campbell was head laundry-maid. But Mary
Campbell was no longer there. She had been
removed when she was taken ill; and as she
would not go into a hospital, according to a preju-
dice familiar among many of her class, lodgings
had been found for her. Thither Hector went
forthwith, into a slummy by-street, where, after
many inquiries, he found the "land" and the
"close" that he sought. He ascended the grimy

and dusky stone stairs. When he had nearly reached the top floor he was met by a short, stout, elderly man, who had just shut a door behind him.

"Is there one Mary Campbell luvvin' here?" he made bold to ask in English.

"Ay, that there is," said the stranger, fixing keen eyes on him. "Are you come for news of her? I am the doctor."

"Yes, yes," Hector said; but he could say no more; his heart was beating like to choke him. He fixed his eyes on the doctor's face.

"Ye'll be one of her Highland cousins, eh? "Ye dinna look like a town-bred lad," said the brusque and burly doctor, with a sort of facetious good-humor. "Well, well, Mary is getting on right enough. Ye might as well go in and cheer her up a bit. The twa lasses dinna seem to have many freens."

"But—but—Flora?" said the forester, with his hungry, haggard eyes still watching every expression of the doctor's face.

"The other one? Indeed, she has had the fever worse than her sister. I wasna sure one night but that she would go——"

MacIntyre seemed to hear no more. Flora was alive—was within a few yards of him. He stood there quite dazed. His eyes were averted; he was breathing heavily. The doctor looked at him for a moment or two.

"Maybe it's the sister you're anxious about?" said he, bluntly. "Weel, she is no out o' the wood yet, but she has a fair chance. What, man, what's the matter wi' ye? It's no such ill news——"

"No, no; it's very good news," Hector said, in an undertone, as if to himself. "I wass— fearing something. Can I see the lass? I wass not hearing from her for a while——"

But he could not explain what had brought him hither. He instinctively knew that this south countryman would laugh at his Highland superstition, would say that his head had been stuffed full of Hallowe'en nonsense, or that at most what he had imagined he had seen and the fact that Flora Campbell had fallen seriously ill formed but a mere coincidence.

"Oh, yes, you can see her," the doctor said, with rough good-nature. "But I'll just go in beforehand to gie her a bit warning. You can talk to her sister for a minute or two. She is sitting up noo, and soon she'll have to begin and nurse her sister, as her sister did her until she took the fever. Come away, lad—what's your name, did ye say?"

"Hector MacIntyre. Flora will know very well where I am from."

The doctor knocked at the door, which was presently opened by a young girl; and while he left Hector to talk to the elder sister, who was lying propped up on a rude couch in a rather shabby little apartment, he himself went into an inner room. When he came out he again looked at Hector curiously.

"Now I understand why you were so anxious," said he, with a familiar smile. "But how came ye to hear she was ill? She says she did not want ye to ken anything about it until she was on the high-road to getting better."

Hector did not answer him. He only looked toward the door that had been partially left open.

"Go in, then," said the doctor; "and dinna stay ower lang, my lad, for she has little strength to waste in talking as yet."

Timidly, like a school-boy, this big strong man entered the sick-room; and it was gently and on tiptoe (lest his heavily nailed boots should make any noise) that he went forward to the bedside. Flora lay there pale and emaciated; but there was a smile of surprise and welcome in the dark blue Highland eyes; and she tried to lift her wasted hand to meet his. What they had to say to each other was said in the Gaelic tongue.

"It is sorry I am to see you like this," said he, sitting down, and keeping her hand in his own. "But the doctor says you are now in a fair way to get better; and it is not from this town I am going until I take you with me, Flora, girl of my heart. The Sutherland air will be better for you than the Greenock air. And your sister Mary will come with you for a while; and both of you will take my little cottage; and Mrs. Matheson will give me a bed at Auchnaver Lodge. I am sure Mr. Lennox would not object to that."

"But, Hector, how did you know that I was ill?" the sick girl said, and her eyes did not leave his eyes for a moment. "I was not wishing you to know I was ill—to give you trouble—until I could write to you that I was better."

"How did I know?" he answered gravely. "It was you yourself who came to tell me."

"What is it that you say, Hector?" she asked, in some vague alarm.

"On Hallowe'en night," he continued, in the same serious, simple tones, "I was at Inver-Mudal. Perhaps I was not caring much for the diversions of the lads and lasses. I walked up the road by myself; and there your wraith appeared to me as clear as I see you now. When I went back and told Mr. Murray, he said 'Did she come forward to you, Hector, or did she go away? She is in great danger. It is a warning; and if she went away from you, you will see her no more; but if she came forward, she is getting better—you will see Flora again.' I knew that myself; but I could not answer him; and my heart said to me that I must find out for myself;

"SHE TRIED TO LIFT HER WASTED HAND TO MEET HIS"

that I must go to seek you; and I set out that
night and walked across the Reay Forest to Loch
Inver, and caught the steamer there. What I
have been thinking since I left Loch Inver until
this hour I cannot tell to you or to any one
living."

"Hector," she asked, "what night was Hallowe'en night? I have not been thinking of such
things."

"It was the night of Tuesday," he answered.

"And that," she said, in a low voice, "was the
night that the fever took the turn. Mary told me
they did not expect me to live till the morning."

"We will never speak of it again, Flora," said
he, "for there are things that we do not understand." And then he added: "But now that I
am in Greenock, it is in Greenock I mean to remain until I can take you away with me, and
Mary too; for Sutherland air is better than
Greenock air for a Highland lass; and sure I am
that Mr. Lennox will not grudge me having a
bed at Auchnaver Lodge. And you will get
familiar with the cottage, Flora, where I hope
you will soon be mistress; and then there will be
no more occasion for a great distance between
you and me; or for the strange things that sometimes happen when people are separated the one
from the other."

NANCIEBEL

A TALE OF STRATFORD-ON-AVON

NANCIEBEL

A TALE OF STRATFORD-ON-AVON

CHAPTER I

"GO FETCH YOUR ALICE HERE"

THERE was a slight sprinkling of snow on this walled and tiled back garden—or back yard, rather—in the High Street of Stratford-on-Avon; and the two figures who, arm-in-arm, were slowly pacing up and down, were well wrapped up, for the night was cold. The one was a tall young fellow of three or four and twenty, of slim build and fair complexion; the other was a young lady of lesser height, who wore a tall hat with tragic sable plumes, and had also a black fur boa wound round her neck. Not much could be seen of her face, indeed, except that she had a pert and pretty nose, and soft, eloquent, pleading dark eyes.

The young man was in an oracular mood. He was delivering a discourse; and it was a discourse

on the letter *h*. He was proving to his companion that all the learned and polished nations of
ancient and modern times had condemned and
despised the letter *h*, even when they did not
resolutely ignore it; and he was insisting that
the importance conferred on that letter by the
English-speaking communities, and the social
use it had been put to, as a sort of shibboleth and
test of one's up-bringing, were the result of nothing but crass and vulgar ignorance.

"Ah! I know what you mean, Richard," the
young lady said plaintively. "It is all to give
me courage—if ever I should meet your mother
some day. For you know, dear, I never do
make a mistake except when I am frightened or
anxious. Indeed," she added shyly, "I think
you are rather sorry, Richard, that you can't
oftener catch me tripping because of the penalty.
You haven't caught me once lately, in spite of
all your difficult sentences. Is that why you in-
stituted prizes instead of penalties? And tell
me this, Richard—how can the same thing be
both a prize and a penalty?"

"Nanciebel," said he, in answer to these mysterious references, "this is not a time for asking
conundrums. I tell you, to-night I am going to
speak to my mother—to tell her the whole
story——"

"Oh, no, Richard," she exclaimed imploringly,

"THE TWO FIGURES WERE WELL WRAPPED UP, FOR THE NIGHT
WAS COLD"

"don't do that! That will only be the end; and we shall never see each other again. And our acquaintanceship has been so pleasant——"

"Acquaintanceship, Nancy!"

"Whatever you like to call it—it has been so pleasant. It will be a thing to look back on in after-years. But it will never be more than that."

"Oh, stuff!" he said, angrily. "I really wonder at you, Nancy! I never get the least help or encouragement from you. Don't I know that the circumstances are difficult enough? But you—you exaggerate them. You haven't the courage of a mouse. You talk as if I were a prince in disguise, and as if you expected my mother to throw you into the Tower as soon as she got to know. I wish you would have a little common sense. The widow and son of a captain in the navy are not such exalted personages——"

At this moment an open door at the foot of the yard was still further opened, and there stood revealed, shining in ruddy light, the stationer's shop and "fancy goods emporium" which was owned by Miss Nancy's elder brother, and over which that young lady herself presided.

"Nancy!" called a small boy—a younger brother.

"All right, Jim! One moment, Richard"—

6

and she had gone to attend to that infrequent
visitor, a customer.

When she had returned, and had taken his
arm again, and nestled up to him (for the night
was exceedingly cold, and she was an affectionate
kind of a creature), she said:

"Richard, what would your mother think if
she saw me behind that counter?"

"She would think you were extremely pretty,"
said he with promptitude; "and what is more,
when she gets to know you, she will say you are
as good, and true, and kind, and warm-hearted
as you are nice to look at.   And what more could
you want?"

"Ah," said Nanciebel sadly, "you fancy she
will see me with your eyes.   But that is not the
way of the world."

"What do you know of the way of the world?"
he made answer.   "Look here, Nancy.   Haven't
I told you that my mother's two books are the
Bible and Tennyson, and that she believes
equally in both?   Very well; now let her put
her faith into practice.   'Kind hearts are more
than coronets, and simple faith than Norman
blood.'"

"Ah, yes; it is so pretty to read about in a
book," said Nanciebel, in her plaintive way, "but
it is so different in actual life——"

He threw away her hand from his arm.

"I have no patience with you!" he said, with an angry frown.

And she on her side was just as quick. She drew herself up, and said with proud lips:

"And I, Mr. Kingston, have no wish to remain here to be insulted. Good-night!"

She was moving haughtily away; and he, in his temper, was like to let her go; but he thought better of it; he put his hand on her shoulder, and somewhat sulkily said, when he laid hold of her:

"Nancy!"

"Oh, I suppose you do not understand," she said, indignantly, "that I have a little self-respect —that I wish to be treated with a little common civility and courtesy? But I would have you know that I am just as proud as you are—prouder —although our stations in life may be different——"

"Nancy!" he said, in a more appealing way.

"But I am content," she continued, in the same proud and indignant tones. "I have asked nothing from you. This relationship between you and me was not of my seeking; and now that it must end—now that it has ended—good and well; I have nothing to regret. Good-night, Mr. Kingston!"

And again she was going away, but he caught her by both shoulders.

"Nancy! Nancy! listen to me! How can you be so unreasonable——"

She tore herself from him; but it was only to burst into a passionate fit of crying and sobbing, her hands over her face, her head averted. Of course he was beside her in a moment, drawing her toward him, and petting her.

"I didn't mean it, Nancy! I meant nothing at all!" he pleaded. "Don't make me miserable! I can't bear to see you crying——"

"It is of no consequence," she sobbed. "It has all come to an end now. I knew it from the beginning. And—and there has been enough of misery—and enough of misunderstanding—and quarrelling—we were never suited for each other —it has been a mistake throughout—and—and now there is an end—and—and I am glad—I am very glad," she said, with another burst of tears.

"Come, come, Nanciebel," said he soothingly and coaxingly, "don't say everything is at an end on the very night that I am going to appeal to my mother, and when I want all the self-confidence and courage I can muster. Why don't you look on the brighter side of things? Think how fond she is of me; she would do anything for me. And then, if it comes to that, I have some claim to be considered. It wasn't nice for me to be called away from Oxford when my father died, at the end of my very first term.

One single term! But did I grudge it? No—not when the mater put it before me, and said how lonely she would be in the world, and asked me to be her companion. And here have I been living in that old-fashioned place, hardly seeing anybody, with next to nothing to do; and when I show my mother how a little family of three would be ever so much more snug and comfortable than our two solitary selves living there, don't you think she will agree?"

"You are so unkind to me, Richard!" murmured Nanciebel, with hidden face; but she did not attempt to get away from him now.

"No, I am not. It is you who are so unreasonable," he protested.

"Then say you will not do it again," the half-sobbing voice murmured.

"I promise you that, or anything else you like, Nancy," he said, "if you'll only look up, and let me see your face, and be good and kind again, as you can be when you choose."

She did as she was bidden; and as she dried her eyes she said:

"I call it downright wicked of you, Richard, when you are about to take such a serious step, to waste the time in quarrelling and trying to vex and hurt me. How do we know how many hours we may ever have together? Perhaps this is the very last, and yet you quarrel——"

"I am sure I did not! It was you!"

"Now, don't begin again, Richard!" she said. "How can you be so unjust, and inconsiderate, and unkind, when you know what I have to suffer for your sake? And are you really going to speak to your mother to-night? When shall I know what she says? Oh, I am so frightened when I think of it! I lie awake at night, wondering how you will begin—wondering what her answer will be. And I know, dear," continued Nanciebel, with a bit of a sigh, "that if she is angry with anybody, it will be with me. She will blame it all on me. She will never think it was you who—who—began to—began to——"

"When once she sees your pretty eyes, Nancy, she will understand the whole affair," said he. "And that is what I am most anxious for. If I can only get her to know you—to know you as you are—I have no fear. It would be all plain sailing then."

"Mothers and sons have different ways of looking at things," said Nancy, who had her little traits of shrewdness, "especially when it is some one the son is fond of. Oh, just to think of going to see her—it frightens me to death! I know what she will be saying to herself: 'You, you impertinent wretch of a girl, how dare you try to entrap my son! How dare you imagine you

will enter our family!' And I don't, Richard,
dear! I don't, indeed. I do not dare to imagine
anything of the kind. I am too terrified. It
would be far better to let everything remain as
it is. You will go and get married to some one
whom your mother will approve of; and many a
year hence you will be saying to your wife: 'I
once knew a girl called Nancy. She lived at
Stratford. I think she was a little bit fond of
me—poor Nancy!' And I suppose I may get
married too; but I wouldn't utter a word to anybody about what is over and gone; I would only
think and think of the dear, dear winter nights
when you used to walk with me arm-in-arm, and
both of us dreaming of all kinds of impossibilities,
and my heart just beating and throbbing for
happiness. And I will never, never part with
the locket—I don't care who may object. If
ever I marry, I will say this: 'Well, you must take
me as I am; and I can't help remembering
things.' And I know this, that whatever happens to me, and whether I marry or don't marry,
the dearest name in all the world will always be
to me—Richard!"

"You speak very freely of the chance of your
marrying some one else," said he (though surely
her artless confession might have been sufficient
for the most exacting of lovers), "but I am going
to make sure you shall do nothing of the kind,

unless you mean to commit bigamy. Is that your little project, Nanciebel?"

"Ah, it is all very well for you to talk with such a light heart, Richard, dear," she answered. "But I don't know what is going to happen to-night, nor what you may have to tell me to-morrow."

"Why, what can happen?" he remonstrated. "You don't understand at all, Nancy. You seem to imagine I am going to face a stern parent, who will storm and rave and cut me off with fourpence-halfpenny, and who will get hold of you and lock you up in a cell on bread and water. My goodness! The mater is just about the gentlest little woman in the world—you will find that out for yourself some day. And why should you dread what is going to happen to-night? Do you think I am going to ask her permission to marry? Not likely! I hope I am old enough to judge and decide and act for myself. But of course when I tell her that I have judged and decided, and that I mean to act on my own account, I hope she will take it all right. It will be so much more pleasant. Of course, I don't wish to annoy her; I wouldn't vex her for the world; and I know I have done nothing to vex her, if she will only listen to reason, and if she will consent to make your acquaintance. For that's where it all

lies, Nancy, as I have told you again and again.
When she knows you she will just take you to
her heart. And that is what I am going to ask
of her to-night—that I may bring you out to
Woodend, so that you two may become friends.
She must know well enough that it is better for
me to marry a good, true-hearted girl, than to
run the racket that most young fellows do; and
where could she find anybody that would make a
more affectionate daughter than yourself, Nancy?
For there is that about you, you know—you
have a fine capacity for loving——"

"You needn't bring that as a charge against
me, Richard!" she interposed with a pout.

"A charge against you! It is your most ador-
able quality, Nancy," he said, "so long as you
reserve all your loving for me. But I shan't
quarrel with you, if you transfer a little of it to
the mater, who can be very affectionate, too,
when she likes. Now, I must be off, dear, or I
shall be late for dinner. To-night I am going
to see what can be done. I think everything
will go smoothly. And to-morrow, how shall I
be able to tell you what has happened? You
know I don't like coming here much in the day-
time, Nancy, lest people should talk."

"Kate will be back from Evesham to-morrow
morning," Nanciebel made answer. "I can get
out at any time. Suppose you meet me at the

end of the church—by the river—that will be out
of the way."

"And at what time, Nancy?"

"Any time you like. Well, say a little after
five o'clock in the afternoon—will that suit you,
Richard?"

Their long and tender adieux over, he passed
through the front premises, and soon he had
quitted the gas-lit streets of Stratford town, and
was out in the white and silent country. As he
strode along the highway, he looked up to the
palely-irradiated heavens, and he repeated aloud
(for he was about as deeply steeped in Tennyson
as his mother was):

> " As shines the moon in clouded skies,
>   She in her poor attire was seen:
>   One praised her ankles, one her eyes,
>   One her dark hair and lovesome mien.
>   So sweet a face, such angel grace,
>   In all that land had never been:
>   Cophetua sware a royal oath:
>   'This beggar-maid shall be my queen!'"

And of course he was the King Cophetua of these
modern times, or at least Nancy appeared to
think so; though she would hardly have appreciated the allusion to her poor attire, for Nanciebel was one of the most smartly-dressed girls in
Stratford-upon-Avon.

And Tennyson was again cunningly called
into requisition that evening by this young man.
When he got home he had just time to dress for
dinner—a mark of respect he never failed to pay
to his mother; then he gave her his arm and led
her into the dining-room as his father had been
wont to do before him. It was a quaint old-
fashioned-looking apartment; for Woodend had
been originally a farm-house, and when it was
changed into an independent residence, they had
transformed the big kitchen into a dining-room;
so that here were stone floors, partially covered
with rugs; and a vast hearth, with brass fire-dogs
for the logs of wood; and shelves over the side-
board for a brave display of shining pewter plat-
ters. Mr. Richard was somewhat silent during
this meal. His mother asked him how he had
spent the day; but he could give no clear account of himself. The fact is, this young man
was accustomed to haunt the town of Stratford
and its neighborhood, on the chance of his getting a glimpse of a certain gray and purple dress
—a costume which he could now recognize at a
great distance, and which told him that Nanciebel
had come forth for a little stroll, perhaps across
the fields to Shottery, or over the bridge and
along to the Weir Brake. It was wonderful what
an amount of conversation these two had to get
through; and how all-important it was that certain

things should be repeated on every occasion on
which they met. Or if they did not speak at all,
they were still happy enough; for their imagina-
tions were busy with the long life-time stretching
out before them. Then, before entering the
town again on their return, they parted (for
Stratford, like most other small places, is inclined
to gossip); and this separation lasted until the
dusk of the winter afternoon came down, and
until the lamps were lit, when he could approach
the little stationer's shop unobserved. At this
time of the year there was not much doing in
any of these establishments. In summer Miss
Nancy was kept busy enough with visitors,
mostly Americans, who bought photographs of
the parish church, of Shakespeare's birthplace,
and of the beautiful river view that has been
spoiled by the hideous theatre, and who were
proud to take away with them as memorials of
their visit all sorts of pen-holders, albums,
needle-cases, blotting-pads, match-boxes, paper-
knives, birthday books, and similar things, each
with a little glazed picture of some bit of Stratford or of Warwickshire to tell where it had come
from. But in winter Miss Nancy's situation was
a sinecure; at any moment she could leave her
sister Kate in charge; nay, if Mr. Richard
chanced to come in of an evening, and if she
was minded to put on her furry jacket and her

tall hat, and go for a little stroll with him up
and down the walled-in inclosure at the back,
even her small brother Jim could take her place,
ready to call out "Nancy" if any one happened
to come in. Jim played gooseberry to perfec-
tion; for he was a studious boy, with a dark love
of pirates, and cut-throats, and equatorial sav-
ages; and when he was revelling in bucketfuls
of blood he little cared how long his sister Nancy
might keep pacing up and down in the crisp
snow out there. Mr. Richard supplied him
bountifully with his favorite literature; and Jim
had eyes and ears for nothing else.

When dinner was over at Woodend, Richard
Kingston went to the door and opened it for his
mother; but ere she passed out on her way to the
drawing-room, he said to her, with his eyes cast
down, and with a most unusual hesitation and
abashment:

"Mother, I want you to do me a favor—I want
you to—to read a page of this book—and—and
to think about it. I have marked it—will you
take it now—and read it?"

"Oh, yes, Richard, of course, if you wish it,"
the gentle-faced little woman said, wondering at
her son's confusion. Had this been a manuscript
poem of his own composition, she could have
understood his embarrassment; but the familiar green volume—her beloved Tennyson—why

should that cause the boy any perturbation?
However, she took away the book with her; and
he shut the door after her and returned to the
fire-place—to stand there and ponder over what
he had done, and its possible consequences.

For the page which Mrs. Kingston had been
besought to read and consider in this especial
manner contained three verses; and the verses
were these:

> " And slowly was my mother brought
>   To yield consent to my desire:
>   She wished me happy, but she thought
>   I might have look'd a little higher;
>   And I was young—too young to wed:
>   'Yet must I love her for your sake;
>   Go fetch your Alice here,' she said:
>   Her eyelid quiver'd as she spake.
>
> " And down I went to fetch my bride:
>   But, Alice, you were ill at ease;
>   This dress and that by turns you tried,
>   Too fearful that you should not please.
>   I loved you better for your fears,
>   I knew you could not look but well;
>   And dews that would have fall'n in tears,
>   I kiss'd away before they fell.
>
> " I watch'd the little flutterings,
>   The doubt my mother would not see;
>   She spoke at large of many things,
>   And at the last she spoke of me;

And turning look'd upon your face,
 As near this door you sat apart,
And rose, and, with a silent grace
 Approaching, press'd you heart to heart."

Would the gentle-eyed and gentle-voiced little
widow in the next room understand? Surely
the message—the entreaty—was clear enough!
Yet he was afraid of his own temerity; and likewise he was afraid that when the time came for
explanation. he could not tell her all that Nanciebel was to him. When ought he to go and see
what impression had been made? Perhaps it
would be more prudent to wait until the first
surprise was over—until she had had time to see
that it was but natural her son should choose for
himself a mate.

As he stood considering, the door was opened,
and his mother appeared. With a sudden sinking of the heart, he noticed that her lips were
pale, and her eyes anxious and concerned. She
shut the door behind her, and came quickly forward, her gaze fixed intently on his face.

"Richard," she said, in an undertone, "who
is she?"

He was startled—and frightened.

"At all events," he said hastily, "you may be
sure of this, that she is worthy to be brought
into this house, and to be received by you as
your daughter."

It was a little speech he had prepared before-hand; but now it did not seem to have any effect.

"Who is she, Richard?" the widow again demanded.

He told her.

"A shop-girl!" she said faintly.

"No, mother, not at all!" he exclaimed eagerly. "The place belongs to her brother, and she merely looks after it for him. He is very well off—you know Emmet & Marlow—he is a watchmaker himself, and I suppose started this other business for the benefit of his two sisters. But what has that got to do with it, mother? She will cease to have any connection with the shop the moment you say the word. And as for herself, there is not a dearer or better girl in the whole country. I am certain you will be the first to say as much when you get to know her——"

"Surely, Richard," the little woman said, in a kind of wistful way, "you might have chosen some one whose family was known to us—who was known to your own friends and relatives. I do not say anything against the girl; it would not be just; but she must herself be aware how strange, how unusual the whole situation is. A clandestine engagement—how came she to consent to that?"

"Mother," said he, taking both her hands in his, "that was all my fault! I ought to have told you long ago; but Nancy was afraid. Cannot you understand—isn't it clear in the poem I asked you to read? Indeed, she was quite in despair; she does not know how gentle, and kind, and considerate you are; she is terrified at the thought of meeting you; indeed, again and again she has told me that what I wished was an impossibility, and that she would never be the means of bringing about any dissension between you and me. Well, I hope that will never arise —she couldn't bear it—she says she would rather give me up a hundred times over——"

The mother looked at her handsome boy.

"Richard," she said, "you know I wish for nothing but your happiness; there is no sacrifice of my own feelings, or my own prejudices, I wouldn't make if I was sure it would make you happy. But consider. Young men of your age are apt to form such fancies. The girl may be everything you say—and yet—and yet it might prove to be only misery for both her and you in the long run——"

"Mother, I want you to see her!" he cried, confident that Nanciebel's soft dark eyes would be sufficient to resolve away all these doubts and fears.

The widow was silent for a moment or two.

"May I bring her to see you, mother?" he entreated.

"Would it be wise, Richard?" she said in reply. "Would not that be making a family compact—would it not be recognizing as a serious engagement what may after all be a mere passing infatuation? Have patience, my dear child; take time; think what a terrible thing it might be to pledge your whole future, and to find out that you had cause to repent. Your Uncle Alexander has often asked you to go out to Shanghai; well, you know how I should grieve to lose you, even for a week or a day; but wouldn't it be wise if you were to go away from Warwickshire for three months or six months, and see whether your mind might not change in the interval? I know what these sudden fancies are worth. They are common to both young men and young women—illusions of the brain—the most uncertain guides. It is for you own sake I speak, dear! You see how I am willing to put aside my own prejudices; it is not because of her station in life that I object; after all, that is not of the first importance. But what surely is of the first importance is that you should know your own minds—that your affection for each other should be tried and found capable of standing the strain of absence. Richard, to please me, will you go out for a few months to Shanghai?"

"Yes, I will, mother," he answered cheerfully and confidently, "if you ask me after you have come to know Nancy a little. Let that be the first thing—then you will be able to judge and decide. Let me bring her to see you!"

The widow hesitated, reluctant; but this handsome lad held her hands in his; and what would she not do for his sake?

"Very well," said she.

He kissed her.

"There is the dearest mother in all the world! Ah, when you and Nancy are friends, you won't talk about Shanghai; you'll be as anxious as I am that she should come and live with you at Woodend. What a pleasant companion for you, mother—so kind, and light-hearted, and loving. I'll tell her, mother! You shall see her to-morrow. And you won't scrutinize her too severely? No, you won't be able—when you look at Nanciebel's eyes!"

CHAPTER II

A PRESENTATION

RADIANT, triumphant, with all the light-hearted hope and courage of youth, Richard Kingston went to keep his assignation with Nanciebel. It had snowed heavily all the preceding night and all the morning; but the afternoon had brightened somewhat, and in the western skies there was now a pale glow of saffron, though that was hardly strong enough to tinge the cold white landscape.

When he reached the church, even-song was going forward; through the windows he could see the gas-jets all lit up—points of lemon-yellow fire in the dusk; and ever and anon came the soft thunder-roll of the organ, and the clear singing of the choir. He walked along to the river-side. The elms overhead were heavily draped with snow, for not a breath of wind was stirring. The dull green surface of the Avon was broken here and there by gray patches of ice floating down with the slow current. On the other side were the flat white meadows; and beyond these again white slopes and heights, with black hedges and trees protruding. The world was quite silent—save for the hushed and slumberous music in the church.

Now, some one had considerately cleared a path from the porch to the side of the stream; so that when Nanciebel came along, the deep snow caused no inconvenience either to her skirts or to her neat, small ankles. It was a cold and cheer-less trysting-place, to be sure; but love's fires burn independently of the weather; and it was not the wintry landscape that was in Miss Nancy's mind.

Nor was it in Mr. Richard's mind either; for now, and quite suddenly and unexpectedly, he experienced a new emotion—an emotion that caused him no little disquiet. Hitherto, when-ever he had caught sight of Nancy, his heart had filled with joy; the most distant glimpse of the gray and purple dress and the sable-plumed hat had been like a kiss for sweetness; his eyes lighted up to welcome her. But now, to his amazement and dismay, he found, as Nanciebel approached, that he was grown anxiously critical. He scrutinized her—her appearance, her expres-sion, her dress, her manner of walking, as if he feared that some objection might be taken. And perhaps she noticed his unusual look as she timidly gave him her hand. She flushed a little; and when she spoke, it was with averted eyes.

"You asked me to meet you, Richard," said she, "and I have come; but not with any kind of expectation. You were too confident. But don't think I shall be annoyed or disappointed; I knew what your mother would say——"

Ah, well, the sound of her voice—with its mys-terious charm, which could thrill his heart with the simplest phrase—that delightful sound gave him courage again; how could his mother withstand those soft, low, penetrating tones? What mattered it what kind of gloves she wore, what kind of brooch was at her neck, when that tender voice could win its way to the heart, when those soft dark eyes could plead for kindness?

"But you're all wrong, Nancy," said he with a kind of forced cheerfulness (for it had alarmed him to find that he could scan the appearance of his sweetheart in this critical way). "The mater wants you to come and see her. It will be all right—as I told you it would. Of course——"

"Of course what, Richard?" she said, seeing he hesitated.

"Well, you can't expect impossibilities, Nancy," said he vaguely.

"Richard," she said, "why don't you confess the truth? Your mother is surprised and grieved by what you have told her; and although she may have said that you might take me to see her, it was against her will, and only to please you. And you know she will never really con-sent, though she may formally do so, out of her fondness for you. Very well; why should you vex and trouble her any more? I say now what I said yesterday. Let this stop where it is. Let us be friends—true friends—always and always —but nothing more than that. Then we can grieve no one."

"And this is what your affection comes to?"

said he reproachfully. "I thought you loved me, Nancy!"

Tears could rise quickly to those dark lashes.

"It is not my fault, Richard," said she. "But everything is against us. I knew your mother would say no——"

"But she does not say no!" he exclaimed. "Nothing of the kind. Of course, as I say, you can't expect impossibilities. You can't expect her to be enthusiastic. What woman would be, about a proposed daughter-in-law she has never seen? It is but natural for her to have doubts. How can she know how thoroughly you and I understand each other? And it is for your happiness as well as mine, that she talks about separation—about the necessity for some considerable time of separation—to see whether we know our own minds. Six months at Shanghai —that's what she proposes for me, Nancy!"

"Shanghai!" repeated Nancy, and she looked up with a frightened stare.

"Yes, indeed. And it's you who have to save me from that banishment. It all rests on your shoulders," he continued more cheerfully. "But I know you will come through the ordeal in triumph. Who could withstand your eyes, Nanciebel? You don't know yourself what a winning fascination they have. And you won't be nervous—after the first second; you will see

my mother wants to be kind. You remember
how the 'Miller's Daughter' was anxious about
what dress would please; but you have nothing
to fear on that score; you are always as neat and
pretty and in good taste as it is possible to be.
I wish I could help you, Nanciebel; but I can't.
You've got to do it all——"

"Richard," said she, a little proudly, "don't
you think it is rather—rather unfair—that I
should be taken out to Woodend on approval?"

"Well, so it would," he answered her, "if anything of the kind were in contemplation. But it
isn't so. You are going out to make the acquaintance of my mother; and you will find her ready
to welcome you, be sure of that. Of course," he
added, in rather a stammering fashion, "I—I
hope you on your side will be—well, conciliatory
—and nice. You need not take it as if it were a
hostile challenge between two women—each anxious to criticise the other. If you go out there
determined to make friends, Nancy, it will be all
right——"

She looked rather blank for a second or
two.

"If I go, it will be for your sake, Richard,"
she said; "but what I am most afraid of is that
I shall be so terrified as to be able to do nothing.
Your mother will think me stiff, or ill-mannered,
or stupid, when I am simply frightened. You

see, you are all impetuosity and eagerness; you don't care; you don't consider what an awkward position I shall be in. It is not as if I were being taken out to visit your mother by some acquaintance knowing us both. I am presented to her all of a sudden, as some one who proposes to become her daughter-in-law. It's nothing to you; you think it is all right and natural; but it is dreadful for me. I know what she will be thinking—that I am a forward, impertinent minx without any delicacy of feeling, or propriety of conduct——"

"Oh, yes," he broke in scornfully. "She is likely to think that of you after she has spoken to you for three minutes! That is precisely your character, Nanciebel; you are so brazen in audacity!"

"And when is this fearful thing to be got through, Richard, dear?" asked Nancy, looking down.

"To-morrow afternoon," he said with ineffable impudence (just as if his mother had made the appointment). "I will bring in the pony-chaise for you, and drive you out."

"But—but where shall I meet you?" she asked again.

"I will come for you," he answered.

"Not into the High Street," she hinted timidly.

"Why not?"

7

"The people would talk," she said with lowered eyes.

"Let them talk," he answered boldly. "It is time this hole-and-corner arrangement was done with. I want the whole thing to be recognized now. When they see Miss Nancy Marlow driving out to Woodend, I dare say they will talk. So much the better! I am not for half-measures."

"No, you never are, Richard," Nancy said, with a bit of a sigh. "And I wonder what will come of it all!"

Nor did she cease to be timorous and apprehensive. It was bad enough that she was going out to Woodend "on approval;" but it was ever so much worse that the neighbors should know it—or guess at it—from the fact of his driving in to the High Street to call for her.

"Don't you think, Richard, dear," said she at last, "it would be better if I met you somewhere a little way out of the town—say at the railway bridge——"

"Then you would have to walk all that way through the snow, Nancy," he pointed out, "and your boots would get wet, or even muddied, if there was a thaw. You see, I want you to be as neat as a new pin, as you always are; not that I care about such things myself; as long as your heart is warm and loving, what do I mind what dress you wear?"

"I understand," Nancy said at once, with quick perception. "You are quite right, Richard. What would your mother say if I went with be-draggled skirts and soiled boots? Of course, of course, you are quite right; you must come for me; and Jim will see that the pavement is dry."

"Have you any white-rose scent for your handkerchief, Nancy?" he asked. "That is the only scent the mater seems fond of. No? Then I'll try and get some, and send it in to you this evening. Oh, you will make a conquest, be sure!"

"What time to-morrow afternoon, Richard, must I be ready?"

"Four: will that do?"

"Very well; now I must be going back into the town. Four o'clock to-morrow afternoon. Oh, dear, I wish it was all over!" said Nanciebel, plaintively.

And perhaps the gentle little widow out there at Woodend had some such thought in her mind when her son told her of this proposed visit on the following day. It is true she knew what was expected of her. Her rôle had been pointed out to her that evening on which Richard had slipped the green volume into her hand. And indeed

she had made up her ·mind that if the girl on
whom he had set his affections seemed to have
an amiable disposition and good manners, she
would not allow the fact of her having stood
behind a counter to influence her mind. So
many young men had done worse! And even if
there were some little defect here or there, some
lack of sensitiveness or refinement, might not
that give way to womanly sympathy and guidance? This little woman was prepared to do a
good deal for her beloved son. Whom else had
she to care for in the world?

And yet, notwithstanding all these kindly and
considerate resolves, and notwithstanding the
diligent coaching that Nanciebel had received
from her sweetheart, it must be confessed that
the meeting between the two women on the
following afternoon was, especially at first, of
the most constrained and ominous kind. Mr.
Richard was so proud of the opportunity of
showing off the beautiful and precious prize he
had won for himself, that he hardly heeded; he
was eager and talkative, and his volubility seemed
in a measure to fill the void of silence that otherwise might have been marked. It is true, he
had been disappointed that his mother and his
chosen bride did not fall upon each other's neck
and weep gentle and sympathetic tears; and he
had been surprised to hear the little widow ad-

dress Nancy as "Miss Marlow;" but he would
not admit to himself that there was any coldness
on either side. Not at all; he was descanting to
his mother on Nancy's general characteristics;
indulging in a little sarcasm even (to give the
whole interview a sort of playful and friendly
cast); but conclusively proving that Nancy and
his mother held precisely the same opinions and
were bound to agree upon every possible subject.
Nancy, for example, was a devoted admirer of
the late Lord Beaconsfield, and did not fail to
wear a primrose on Primrose Day. Nancy believed that the honor of the country was safe in
the hands of the Conservative party, and that
Radicals, and Socialists, and atheists, and people of that sort had nothing in view but the
destruction of property and the total abolition
of law. Nancy was a devout adherent of the
Church of England, and considered it unbecom-
ing, if not positively dangerous, for bishops to
have any dealings with the Dissenters. Nancy
strongly disapproved of women's-right women.
Nor was Nancy quite sure about the influence of
the school boards, which she considered apt to
draw away the children from their proper and
natural guardians and friends, who had always
been good to them in times past. Nancy detested
the use of cosmetics, and wondered that respectable girls in London could condescend to such

practices. As to tight lacing, Nancy was also
sound; who but a fool would want to sing, "I'd
be a butterfly?" In short, it was Nancy, and
Nancy, and Nancy all the time; why should any
one speak of Miss Marlow?

But here a significant little incident occurred
which showed how very differently mother and
son viewed this position of affairs. When Nanciebel was ushered into the drawing-room, Mr.
Richard insisted on her laying aside her hat and
jacket and gloves, so that she should have the
appearance of being quite at home; and then he
conducted her to a little windowed recess at the
top of the room which his mother used as a boudoir. It was a remarkably snug and cozy apartment, a couch running round three sides of it;
shelves of books covering two of the walls; the
windows commanding a view of the garden,
where thrushes and blackbirds and starlings were
hunting about among the snow for the food
which the widow was wont to fling abroad with
a generous hand. It would have pleased Mr.
Richard if his mother and his sweetheart, on
entering this secluded little place, had sat down
together, perhaps arm-in-arm; but somehow Miss
Marlow took her seat on one side, where she remained looking amiable and attentive if somewhat
silent, while Mrs. Kingston, on the couch opposite her, listened to her son's dithyrambics or

glanced out upon the wintry garden as she
spoke. And what now happened was this.
Mr. Richard, having conclusively shown that
Miss Marlow's mental and moral qualities, and
her opinions on political, religious, and social
subjects generally, were such as to commend her
to any intelligent and reasonable human being,
proceeded, in a sort of half-playful and kindly
way, to say something of the young lady's appearance. You see, she appeared to be already
one of the family. Here she was, in the snug
little corner, not with hat and gloves on, as
though she were paying a formal call, but as if she
had just come down from her own room to have
a little chat before tea was brought in. And
thus it was that when Mr. Richard, chancing to
talk of the fashion in which his beloved wore her
hair, went on to suggest that perhaps it might
suit her better to wear it a little higher on her
forehead, he quite naturally and unthinkingly
crossed over to her, and with a light touch or two
of his fingers pushed back her hair, so as to in-
vite his mother's opinion. But the reply he received startled him.

"Richard!" the widow exclaimed, in amazed
protest; and then all at once he knew how
differently his mother and he were regarding this
young lady. Not yet was she the daughter of
the house, to be treated with familiar little caress-

ings and pettings; she was only a visitor, she
was only Miss Marlow, to be treated with deco-
rum and respect. As for poor little Nancy, she
was terribly embarrassed. Richard, she knew,
should not have taken this liberty; but he had
done it almost before she was aware, and indeed
it was not until afterward she bethought her of
what Mrs. Kingston might guess from this little
incident. Mr. Richard did not try any more ex-
periments with Miss Marlow's hair, or seek to
alter the way in which it lay on her forehead.
He returned to his seat with an uneasy consciousness that he had made a mistake—and perhaps
even compromised Nancy a little; but fortunately
at this moment tea was brought in, and that
proved to be a welcome distraction.

For in truth, the widow, critical as she might
be of her son's choice, could hardly help sympa-
thizing with the girl in the lonely and embarrassing position in which she was placed; and then
again, Nancy, though shy and silent, was obvi-
ously most anxious to please. Once, indeed, in
answer to a question, she said, " Yes, ma'am;"
and although Mr. Richard inwardly winced—for
the phrase recalled the shop and the counter—his
mother did not appear to look on it in that light.
Perhaps it was a kind of pathetic confession of
humility; perhaps it was a kind of tribute to the
widow's dignity; and every one knows how peo-

ple who are not gifted with any great magnificence
of manner are pleased when they think they im-
press.

Moreover, when, in the general talk that now
ensued round the tiny tea-table, there was any
possibility of a difference of opinion, Mr. Richard
adroitly managed that his mother and Nancy
should be on the same side, while he challenged
their combined forces from the other. Take the
question of Mops, for example. The Mop in
Stratford-on-Avon, as in some other old English
towns, is a hiring fair at which farm-servants,
men and women, come in from the surrounding
country to offer their services to master or mistress; and for the refreshment of these stout-
stomached folks, or any other who may be of a
like mind, oxen and pigs are roasted in the prin-
cipal thoroughfares—the hungry yokel paying
for a slice off whatever portion of the slow-revolv-
ing animal may take his fancy, and carrying
the smoking plate into the adjacent public-house,
where he can wash down the beef or pork with
copious draughts of ale. Now, there are those
who hold that this roasting of a huge carcass
and the public ladling of gravy is a brutalizing
spectacle; and they would have that feature of
the Mop suppressed, even if the other concomi-
tants—the merry-go-rounds, the boxing booths,
the rifle galleries, and what-not—were allowed

to remain. This was Mrs. Kingston's opinion; and Mr. Richard cunningly contrived that it should be Nanciebel's also.

"Oh, I think the old-world customs should be preserved," said he boldly, "so long as they don't involve cruelty to animals—and you don't put an ox to shame by roasting it in public. They talk of asking the magistrates to suppress the Mop altogether—so that I suppose they wouldn't even allow the men and women to come into the town with a bit of straw stuck in their cap, or whatever other symbol it is that tells the farmer what kind of work the applicant wants. Well, I think it is a pity; I think the old cere-monies and customs should be preserved——"

"The roasting of these animals in the streets seems to me simply horrid," his mother said.

"Well, I know that is Nancy's opinion, too," he said (Nancy never having uttered a single word to him at any time on the subject). "And I don't wonder she should refuse to go through the streets on the day of the Mop. The smell of the cooking is rather too pronounced. Still, there is no reason why fastidious people like you and Nancy should go near at all. You may keep away. Give the bucolics their holiday, in the manner they can enjoy it; roasting animals has always been a sign of rejoicing; it is a testimony —in fact, you can see it only too plainly, if you are walking along Chapel Street—that there is fat in the land."

"Don't, Richard!" his mother said, with a piteous expression; and he was quite willing to abandon the controversy—leaving his mother and Nanciebel on the winning side together.

Well, the visit came to an end at last; and Mrs. Kingston bade good-by to Nancy without a word having been said on the subject which was, no doubt, uppermost in both their minds. Nor was there any parting embrace; nor the slightest recognition of the peculiar circumstances that had brought about this interview. None the less was Mr. Richard triumphant as he drove away his chosen bride through the melting snow.

"What do you say now, Nanciebel?" he demanded. "Didn't everything go off first-rate?"

"O Richard, I am just dying of shame," she murmured, and she wouldn't look at him.

"Why, what is the matter?" he asked in astonishment. "I thought everything went off most satisfactorily; there wasn't a slip or mistake anywhere, unless it was my own when I took to rearranging your hair. That did stagger the mater, I admit."

"Richard," said she, "didn't you notice? When you asked me in the hall if I had got my gloves, I said, 'Yes, dear.' The next moment I thought I should have sunk through the floor with shame and mortification."

"I'm sure I did not notice it," he said.

"But your mother did—I saw her look."

"Very well, then—a good thing too! Why should she not know the actual relations that exist between us? Now that I think of it, I am not sorry that I raised your hair a little bit on your forehead, and tried the effect of it, as if you already belonged to me. No, I am not sorry. It is better she should know; then she will understand the intimacy of our relationship, and the length of time it has lasted. I have no doubt she thought it was only a passing fancy. That was why she talked of Shanghai. There was no mention of Shanghai this afternoon."

"No, Richard, for she seemed careful not to admit that she understood there was anything between you and me," said Nanciebel, who was a good deal less confident than her lover. "She treated me just like a stranger—but very kindly, I must say that. And—and I am not nearly so afraid of her as I was," Nanciebel added.

"Afraid of her!" he repeated, with a laugh. "Why, you two will be the fastest friends in the world within a couple of months from now. I told you she would not be able to resist you. She seemed pleased with you throughout; and

you never in your life looked prettier or more
winning—that I know."

Nanciebel shook her head.

"A woman understands a woman's ways of
looking and talking," she said. "If ever she
does give her consent, it will be simply and
solely for your sake, Richard. She does not
like me."

"Nancy!"

"Ah, but I know," said Nanciebel doggedly.
"I don't suppose she positively hates me—for I
gave her no occasion by provoking a quarrel or
anything of that kind; but I dare say she is crying at this moment, and wishing in a sort of way
that I had never been born."

"And you think that is the impression she
formed of you, Nancy?" he asked. "I tell you,
you are too diffident. You don't know your own
value. Of course she couldn't say anything—to
your face. But wait till I get home this evening,
then she will speak; and be sure, when I next
see you, I shall be able to tell you something that
will banish all those idle fears and surmises.
You think you could judge by her expression?
Well, then, you have made a bad guess, my dear
Nancy—as I will prove to you to-morrow."

She was for getting out of the pony-chaise at
some point on the Alcester Road, so that she

might walk into the town on foot; but he would not hear of any such thing; he cared not who might know he had won his bride; he drove through Stratford, and along the High Street, and up to her own door. As he bade her good-by, he said he would call and see her the next day; he expected to have some news to tell her—as the result of this memorable interview.

But as he drove leisurely home through the gathering dusk, he was not quite so confident as he had professed to be while talking to Nanciebel. It was strange that his mother had not kissed the girl in taking leave of her. That would have been sufficient recognition. Her parting little speech to the effect that she hoped Miss Marlow would come and see her again might have been addressed to the merest stranger. As for Nancy's contention, on the other hand, that she could tell that Mrs. Kingston disliked her, and had even the monstrous inhumanity to wish that she were dead—he knew that was all nonsense. However, there would soon be an opportunity for him to learn what had been his mother's thought.

During dinner nothing of importance was said with regard to Nanciebel; for old Thomas, who looked after the pony and kept the garden and also waited at table, was continually coming and going. But after dinner, Mr. Richard went direct with his mother into the drawing-room, and sat down beside her, and took her hand, and smoothed it between his own.

"Now, mater, what are you going to say to me?"

The little woman hesitated; it was a momentous crisis in her simple and uneventful life.

"What can I say to you, Richard?" she said rather sadly. "I do not wish to appear unkind or inconsiderate. But—you must surely understand how it must be a shock to me to know that I am expected to receive a stranger into our home——"

"A stranger, mother!" he exclaimed. "How long would she be a stranger?"

"And then, my dear boy," continued the mother in the same absent way, "I have been building up so many forecasts of your future— and this is so entirely different. However, we must do what is right—we must do what is right, whatever it may cost. Much as I should like to see you free from this—this entanglement, I would not have you win your freedom through any dishonorable action. If you have raised hopes in this young woman's heart—if you have pledged your word to her, you must stand by that. I would not have your conscience burdened by the knowledge that you had trifled with her, and cruelly forsaken her; no, not if I was

thrice as anxious you should look elsewhere for
a wife——"

"Why, I knew you would say that, mother!"
he cried joyfully, though his exultation was in
curious contrast with the widow's half-concealed
regret. "And then, consider this—if you found
her passably agreeable, and pleasant-mannered,
and amiable, on a first and formal interview like
that—just consider how she will improve, how she
will win your regard on more intimate knowledge.
What did you think of her, mother? Weren't
you favorably impressed? I'm sure you must
have thought she looked so pretty and neat and
modest. Did you notice how soft and winning
her eyes were? Couldn't you guess what her
disposition was like? At all events, she tried
hard to please you. I could see it in every look."

"I have no fault to find, Richard," his mother
said, but without much of the enthusiasm he had
hoped for. "I dare say she is a good, honest
girl, and may make you a good wife—if only—if
only she had some little instruction—and prep-
aration——"

"Mother, Nancy is the quickest girl in apprehension you ever saw!" he exclaimed eagerly.
"I don't know in what you consider her deficient,
but I know she would be delighted to learn—and
especially from you. Didn't you see how re-
spectful she was to you?" he continued with

insidious flattery. "She would be a most willing pupil. Of course you saw she was shy—that was but natural in a girl of her age, and in the peculiar circumstances. You could not expect her to have your self-possession and grace of manner; that is something that can only be acquired by long training—but how willingly Nancy would try to learn!"

"It is all so strange to me as yet, Richard," Mrs. Kingston said at length, "that I hardly know what to do. But in such an important matter I cannot act entirely on my own responsibility. I will write to your uncle Charles. Perhaps he will run up from Bristol."

"Mother!" Mr. Richard protested, with some indignation. "Do you want to frighten poor Nancy out of her senses? A family conclave—a jury of strangers to summon the poor girl before them——"

"You cannot call your uncle Charles a stranger," his mother retorted, but without asperity; this alarming thing that had happened had stunned and frightened her rather than made her angry. "Who, after myself, could have your interests more at heart? And I have been thinking, Richard, that if you still persist in this project—or if you are bound in honor to Miss Marlow—then perhaps your uncle Charles would receive her into the vicarage for a while and

let her associate with your girl-cousins. A clergyman's house is the best school in the world for
any one who wishes to pick up the ways and
manners, the little courtesies and politenesses of
refined society. And I am sure the separation
would be wholesome for both you and her; it
would give you time to reflect; it would enable
you to test the strength of your regard for each
other. Now, Richard, dear, don't ask me to say
anything more, until I have consulted with your
uncle. I am sure that our chief and only consideration will be your happiness."

That silenced him, of course; he could plead
and urge no further. But when he thought of
his having to communicate this new scheme to
Nancy on the next day, his heart sank within
him. Poor Nanciebel!

———

CHAPTER III

"ADIEU, MY DEAR!"

IN reply to the widow's letter, the Rev. Charles
Henningham came up from Bristol forthwith; he
was not one to underestimate the gravity of such
a crisis in the family affairs. He was a small,
thin, nervous, pale-faced man, with large, almost

feminine eyes, and with a manner as gentle and delicate as that of his sister. Like her, too, in this particular instance, he never for a moment thought of repudiating the obligations under which his nephew Richard had placed himself— not at all; if the young man had pledged his word to an honest and honorable girl, he must stand by it, and his family must simply try to do the best in the circumstances.

Mr. Richard was not at home when his uncle arrived, so that there was a little preliminary conversation between brother and sister—of course about Nanciebel.

"I presume, Cecilia," said the nervous little clergyman, in his softly-modulated tones, "that she has none of the accomplishments one would naturally wish Richard's wife to have?"

"Indeed, I never thought of questioning Richard on that point," Mrs. Kingston said, "for I supposed she would merely have the ordinary education of one in her sphere of life. Of course she can read and write and figure up accounts; but beyond that, what? Not that I put much value myself on young-lady accomplishments. A girl can get on very well without Italian, and French, and German, and music, if she has a good manner, and can write a clever letter, and play lawn-tennis. But really, this girl on whom Richard has set his heart has no manner at all.

That afternoon she was here, she had absolutely nothing to say for herself. And you know how popular Richard is, Charles; his good looks and high spirits stand him in good stead everywhere; and to think of his being joined for life to this— this—well, I will say nothing against her—but I cannot help regarding it as a cruel misfortune."

"We must make the best of it, Cecilia," said the clergyman with chastened reisgnation; "and you may count on me to do what I can. If you think she would gain any improvement by coming to the vicarage for a few months—or even for a year, if you consider a lengthened period of separation advisable—I shall be glad to take her, and she might join Gertrude and Laura in their studies as far as that is practicable. You say she appears amiable and sincere; and I am sure if there was any objectionable feature in her character, she would not have been Richard's choice."

"It would be the greatest kindness, Charles," the widow said, with obvious gratitude. "It might not be practicable for her to join your girls in their studies—they are too far advanced—and it would be too late in the day for her to begin music now; but she might practise her handwriting until she acquired a good style; and they might teach her lawn-tennis. But above all, what I should hope for is her gaining a little more self-confidence and frankness—familiarity with good manners—and so forth; and where could she find two more charming girls to observe and copy than Gertrude and Laura? Of course it will be a difficult thing to propose to her, without wounding her susceptibilities. We can't tell her that she is ill-educated, or gawky in manner, or unacquainted with the ways and politeness of a well-bred family ; it will be easier to point out the necessity for some period of separation, as a test of their regard for each other. And I hope she will understand that it is done in kindness; for after all, if she is to be Richard's wife, I trust she will bear no grudge against any one of us."

"She would be a very ungrateful young woman if she did," said the clergyman, with unusual severity, "considering the very great sacrifices we are all of us prepared to make for her."

And what did Nanciebel say to this scheme when it was laid before her? It was Mr. Richard who communicated it to her. On the day following his uncle's arrival he called in at the shop in the High Street, and asked Nancy to come for a stroll with him; and as her sister Kate was there, she consented; and the two of them walked along Chapel Street and Church Street without the slightest pretence of concealment. The temporary thaw had been succeeded by hard frost;

the snow again lay crisp and clear, while the
roads glittered with broken ice in the cart-ruts.
There was a blue sky overhead; it was a bright,
inspiriting morning; these young folks had no
thought of the cold. They passed the church;
they went down by the mill; they ascended the
slippery steps of the foot-bridge, and there, lean-
ing on the rail, they paused to look at the sluggish green river, or at the wide white snow-land-
scape all shining in the sun. And here it was
that he told her what his mother and uncle
proposed should be done.

"O Richard," she said, when his tale was
finished, "that is as bad as your going to Shanghai!"

"Well, it is not, Nanciebel!" he made answer.
"For I should be allowed to go down and see
you from time to time; and it is easier sending
messages or birthday presents, or things of that
kind, between Stratford and Bristol than between
Stratford and Shanghai. But the great difference
is this: my uncle Charles, with whom you would
be staying, is one of the gentlest and kindest of
men, whereas my uncle in China, from what I
can remember of him, is one of the most fiery
and ill-tempered—a regular pepper-caster. You
see, both the mater and I have grievously
offended him. He has been talking for ever
so long back of retiring—he has made a large

fortune; and he has always been anxious that I
should go out and become a junior member of
the firm: I suppose he could make that one of his
conditions. Well, you know, the mater wanted
me at home; and besides, I have no turn for
business; and at home I have stayed. I dare
say he considers us a couple of fools. But if I
were to go out to Shanghai, and if he were to dis-
cover that I hadn't come with any intention of
studying Pekoe and Souchong, but only to be
kept away for a while from a too fascinating
young lady in Warwickshire, then there would
be an explosion! I should have a remarkably
lively time of it during that six months! Whereas you, Nanciebel, you will be with the very
nicest people you could wish for; and they will
be very kind to you, for my mother's sake; and
I will write to you every day—that is to say, if I
am only allowed to send you one letter a week,
that can't prevent my writing every day, and
sending you the whole budget on Saturday. Do
you see, Nanciebel?"

"Well, I don't understand yet, Richard," said
Nanciebel, gazing mournfully at the green river,
with its slow-moving patches of ice, "I don't understand why they should want us to be separated, unless it is in the hope of the separation
being forever."

"How can you say that, Nancy?" he protested.

"Why, isn't it on the distinct understanding that you are to be my wife that the mater has made this proposal and that my uncle asks you to make his house your home? Would they take all this trouble for nothing? Then there's another thing, Nanciebel. If I were dealing with a stern and truculent parent, threatening and bullying, I might be tempted to show fight; I should probably say, 'I have chosen my wife, and stamping and roaring won't alter the fact. You say you will cut me off with a shilling?—well, go and do it, and be hanged to you!' But, you know, Nancy, you couldn't use language like that to such a gentle creature as the mater; and as for cutting me off with a shilling, no one threatens to do that, for the simple reason that no one has the power: when I am twenty-five, some eighteen months hence, I come into my little money, and am my own master. So that in the mean time, Nanciebel, why should you grumble over our being separated for a while?"

"It seems to me, Richard," said Nanciebel, with a pout, "that you take this separation very easily. I believe you are glad to get rid of me."

"Oh, yes, certainly," said he, sidling closer to her as they leaned over the rail of the bridge. "That is extremely probable. Have you made any other discovery, Nancy?"

"Well, how would you like it yourself?" she

asked abruptly. "How would you like to be taken away from your own family—as if they weren't good enough for you to associate with—and sent to live among strangers?"

"If you mean being sent to live at Holiwell Vicarage, I should like it amazingly," said he, with a jovial air. "My cousins are awfully nice girls—and extremely pretty, too. I shouldn't object, not in the least!"

She moved away from him, and remained silent.

"Come now, Nanciebel," he said, following her, "don't be sulky. Tell me I may say to my mother that you will consider this scheme, and that if your brother has no objection, you will do what she wants."

"No," said Nanciebel, distinctly, "I refuse. I am not going to tell my family that they are no longer good enough for me. I refuse; that is my answer. You can go down to Bristol, if you like; if you prefer your cousins to me, you are welcome!"

"I never said anything of the kind," he exclaimed.

"You did, and you said you would be glad to be rid of me——"

"Nancy!"

"It is mean of you—downright mean of you," she said in indignant tones, "to deny having said certain things simply because you did not use such

8

and such words. What you intended to say is
quite enough for me—thank you! And I have
had enough—all the way round. I wish to have
done with such treatment—once for all. I am
going home."

She moved proudly away; but he accompanied
her. Then she stood stock-still.

"I wish to go alone," she said with firm lips.

"I shan't allow you," he said (not dreaming
there was anything serious in the wind). "I
know better than you what is good for you,
Nancy; I am going back with you."

She remained undecided for a moment—vexed
and mortified and helpless. Then she said
slowly and bitterly:

"I have often heard that one may be born in
the position of a gentleman without having the
manners or feelings of a gentleman, but I had
never seen it before. I should have thought
that a gentleman would respect my wish."

"No, no, Nanciebel," said he, shaking his
head, "the tragedy-queen does not become you.
You're not tall enough, not fierce enough. Are
you going to give me your hand?"

An implacable determination was on her
mouth.

"I wish to pass," said she stiffly (though he
was not barring the way at all). "And I wish
to go back home alone."

Then quick as flame his mood changed.

"Oh, go home alone, then!" he said with frowning brow; and the next moment he had turned from her and was striding eastward along the bridge, leaving Nanciebel to get down the slippery steps and make her way home as she pleased.

As for him, he struck off through the snow-covered meadows, caring little whither he went, but vowing vengeance all the time. She was too unreasonable! He would suffer this kind of thing no longer. Here were both his mother and his uncle doing everything they could think of for her—not spurning her and refusing to receive her into the family, as many would have done, but laying thoughtful and kindly plans and schemes to assure her a happy future; and she must needs break out into a fit of temper, and flatly decline to accept their good offices. It was too outrageously unreasonable! He would teach her a lesson this time. She would have to come humbly to him, and promise amendment before he would permit of any reconciliation. Nanciebel would find out that he was not to be trifled with.

Alas! for these brave resolutions; the first thing he saw on returning to Woodend was a small packet addressed to himself lying on the hall table. He opened it—hurriedly and anxiously—for he had recognized the handwriting. Here were a bundle of letters, and one or two tiny packages carefully wrapped up; likewise the following note:

"RICHARD: I return you your letters, and also the presents you have given me.   Good-by.
                                   "NANCY."

He stared in alarm and bewilderment.   Did she mean it?   Had she taken mortal offence because of the imagined slight to her family—a slight that he ought to have explained away? Perhaps she had consulted her elder brother before taking this serious step!   And then (with a jump of the heart) he observed that before the word "*letters*" in the above note she had originally written "*dear*," but had scored that out.   The obliteration had been done but lightly; perhaps she had meant him to see the little adjective after all?   He was not so angry with Nanciebel now. It was her love that had dictated that little word of four letters, if it was her pride that had compelled her to score it out again.

Toward dusk on the same afternoon, Mr. Richard again made his appearance in the High Street.   Nanciebel blushed furiously when he entered the shop; there was a curious look in her eyes, moreover; his heart smote him—he guessed she had been crying.

"I want to speak to you, Nancy," he said, in a grave voice.

Her sister Kate was behind the counter, busy with her needle; so, without more ado, Nancy drew a shawl round her shoulders, and passed into the back garden, leaving the door open. He was at her side in a second.

"Will you take back the letters, Nancy?" said he rather hesitatingly, for he knew not in what mood she might be. "You cannot mean what you say. It isn't all over between us because— because of a quarrel. And I'm sure I had no intention of saying or hinting that your family were not good enough for you to associate with— no such intention in the world."

"O Richard," she suddenly said in a voice full of pathetic appeal, "do be good to me! It quite breaks my heart when there is anything wrong between you and me! I will do what you want. I will do everything your mother wishes, only—only—be kind to me, Richard!"

The next instant his hands were clasped round her soft dark hair; her eyes were upturned to his.

"Why aren't you always like this, Nancy?" he said.

"Because you won't let me," she said plaintively. "But don't begin again, Richard! Have you—have you brought the letters—and the locket and the other things?"

He took the little package from his pocket and handed it to her; she furtively kissed it ere transferring it to her own.

"So you will go to Bristol, Nanciebel?"

"Yes, dear!" she said, looking down again.

"And do you imagine I don't understand what you are thinking—or dreading? And of course I sympathize with you all the same, even if I know your fears are groundless. Why, they will be as kind to you as it is possible for you to wish! It isn't as if you were going as a governess into a strange house where the daughters might bully you, and the servants try to snub you; you are are going to a home—to be received as my future wife; and the chief points of education that the mater seems to have in view are lawn-tennis and the way of dressing your hair—though I fancy you could give Gerty and Laura a lesson in that, rather than they you. It seems to me that it will be simply a holiday for you—a long holiday——"

"Yes, Richard, long—now long?" she interposed.

"They were talking about a year," he answered evasively.

"Ah, well," she responded, with a submissive sigh, "I suppose if I have promised to do everything your mother wishes, there is no more to be said. But it will be dreadful, Richard—never

seeing you. I shall lose heart, I know. I have
heard of people pining and moping until they fell
into an illness; well, if that should happen to
me, perhaps I shall not be sorry. I have only
been in the way—and a cause of trouble. But if
anything were to happen to me—when I was far
from my friends, and from you, and from any
one I cared for, I should have the consolation of
knowing that I had done everything that had
been asked of me; and I suppose your mother
and your uncle would have no ill feeling toward
me then; and you — you wouldn't quite forget Nanciebel — sometimes you would remember——"

There was a sob in the dark.

"Come, come, Nancy," said he soothingly,
"you needn't have any such apprehensions.
And you are not going to be left alone like that.
I shall stipulate for being allowed to go down
and see you once at least in every two months—
they talked of three months——"

"Couldn't it be every month, Richard?" she
pleaded.

"Nanciebel," said he, "you'd begin to think
me a nuisance. Why, you'll be so busy with
your amusements and excursions and all the
charitable work connected with the vicarage that
you'd resent my coming bothering you so often.
However, that can all be arranged afterward.

You will find the mater most considerate; she
will agree to anything you ask; and don't
imagine you are going to banishment or impris-
onment—but to have a long and pleasant holiday, in a nice house, among the most friendly
people in the world."

That night at dinner Mr. Richard informed
his mother and his uncle that Miss Marlow had
given her consent to the scheme which had been
placed before her, and pathetically tried to draw
from them some expression of sympathy or approval.   But the widow received the news with
a grave reserve; perhaps in her secret heart she
had been wondering whether Nanciebel might
not definitely refuse and so prepare the way for
a rupture of the engagement.

"I hope it will all turn out well, Richard," the
mild-voiced clergyman said, "and I am sure myself and the girls will do what we can to make
the young lady feel at home.   We must simply
agree to regard her as already one of the family.
But sometimes I wonder what your uncle Alexander will say when he comes to hear of it."

"My uncle Alexander," said Mr. Richard, with
some independence, "seems to think he owns
me, simply because he happens to have been my
father's brother.   But I do not see that I am so
much beholden to him.   I hardly know him, to
begin with; and he has done nothing for me—ex-

cept to make offers he must have known I could not accept——"

"He might do a great deal for you," the widow said. "He has made a large fortune——"

"Yes, but of course he'll leave it all to that girl, his step-daughter. She is the only one who has any claim on him—I don't consider I should look to him for anything——"

"Well, you needn't," his mother said sadly, "after he hears of what has now taken place."

"What I look to him for," said Mr. Richard with some firmness (for well he knew what view the irascible old gentleman out in Shanghai would take of this matter), "is to mind his own affairs, and not interfere where he is not wanted. He writes about me," he continued, addressing his uncle, "as if I were a child, and as if the mater were a nursery-governess neglecting her duty. Well, I won't have it. He hasn't acquired the right to intermeddle——"

"He has been most kind and thoughtful," Mrs. Kingston pleaded. "If his remonstrances were sometimes couched in plain language, surely, my dear boy, you must have known what his intentions were. Again and again he has offered to give you a place in the firm; and if I have been selfish enough to ask you to relinquish these chances, and to stay at home with me, it hasn't been always with a good conscience."

8*

"Well, well, mother," her son replied, "it is no use talking about that now. I am not going out to Shanghai. And I don't want any of Uncle Alexander's money; let it go to my cousin who is not my cousin—Florence her name is, isn't it?"

Now the Rev. Mr. Henningham had to return to Bristol the next day; but it was hardly to be expected that Nanciebel could accompany him on such short notice. She would wish to say good-by to her friends and relatives; moreover, her wardrobe might require looking after, seeing that she was to be away for so long; and Mrs. Kingston undertook that the young lady should arrive at Holiwell Vicarage fully equipped. Nanciebel had again been persuaded to pay an afternoon visit to Woodend; and although she was quite as shy and nearly as silent as on the previous occasion, nevertheless her neat appearance and becoming modesty made a favorable impression on the clergyman, while Mrs. Kingston, now fully recognizing the course of events as inevitable, made less constrained advances toward friendliness and intimacy. Mr. Richard seemed highly pleased with the result of this interview. It all seemed settled now. And Nancy no longer appeared to be afraid. That period of banishment was not to be so dreadful, after all.

In the mean time Uncle Charles had nobly undertaken the duty of calling upon Nanciebel's elder brother, in order to explain to him the position of affairs, and what were their plans for the future. It was a most delicate and invidious task. For when two young people become engaged, their friends and acquaintances—and even the world at large—charitably and amiably assume that the young lady has had nothing whatever to do with bringing about this result; it is the young man who is solely and wholly responsible. Accordingly the question remained as to how Nanciebel's brother would regard this spiriting away of his sister. Doubtless he would assume that *she* was innocent of any preliminary flirtation; she had not replied to stolen glances, or let her hand part reluctantly from his, or indulged in any sort of sly and innocent coquetry. No, no. She had been pursued with attentions; flattered; coaxed; finally, out of her generous good-nature, she had given consent—to the young man who was now answerable for the whole affair. As the good clergyman made his way to the shop of Emmet & Marlow, watchmakers and silversmiths, he became a little anxious. If young Marlow had taken that stationer's business chiefly as a means of providing employment for his sisters, he might be willing enough to have the maintenance of one of the girls taken off his hands. If, on the contrary, he had embarked in the enterprise as a speculation on his own account, he might object to have his manageress carried off in this peremptory fashion. Much would depend on his personal disposition; and Mr. Henningham, who was a peaceable and timid little man, hoped at least that young Marlow would not turn out to be a fierce and angry Radical, indignant at the thought of his sister being borne away into captivity in order to become the bride of a scion of the so-called upper classes.

Mr. Henningham was speedily reassured. Nanciebel's brother he found to be a respectable, quiet-mannered, sensible young man, who spoke wtih equal intelligence and frankness.

"No, sir," he said respectfully to the clergyman, "I did not like your nephew coming about the place at all. I would have stopped it if I had known in time. I think Nancy ought to marry in her own circle. However, I suppose it is no use talking about that now. Well, I think your proposal is very generous; and I see good reasons for it; the only thing is that you must allow me to pay for my sister's board."

"My dear sir," said the clergyman blandly, "I hope you will not raise the question. I think both Mrs. Kingston and myself would prefer to regard your sister as already one of the family——"

The young man flushed.

"Oh, I can't have Nancy go anywhere as a beggar," said he, but without rudeness. "Once she is married it will be different."

"We will waive the point at present, then," said Mr. Henningham, who was extremely pleased to have got over this awkward interview so easily; and, as he was going away, he was good enough to say: "And, of course, you understand that while we consider this period of separation a wholesome thing as between those young people, we have no wish to restrict Miss Marlow's full and free intercourse with her own relatives; and if her sister or yourself were at any time anywhere near Bristol, I should be only too pleased to see you at Holiwell Vicarage."

Uncle Charles went away down again into Somersetshire to tell his daughters whom they were to expect. Then a week or two went by, during which Nanciebel was preparing for her departure. Then came the night of farewell (for she was going off by train next morning), and Nancy and her lover were, as on many a previous occasion, strolling arm-in-arm up and down the little tiled court-yard.

"Life is so much harder in reality," Nanciebel was saying in a rather sad way, "than it is in things you read of in books. I thought it was kind of your mother to give me Tennyson's

Poems yesterday, Richard. She told me how it was you asked for her consent; and how she couldn't refuse; and when I came home, I read the poem all over again. But everything went so easily for the Miller's Daughter. A single interview with the young man's mother: that was all. There was no talk of sending her away from her friends—to live with strangers—perhaps for a whole year. You say they are not strangers, Richard, dear; and, of course, they are not to you, but they are to me. And the life will be strange. I know I shall feel dreadfully lonely. I shall spend half the night crying——"

"No, no, no, Nanciebel!" he said. "You don't know what you are talking about. It will be a far pleasanter life for you than your present one——"

"Without you, Richard!" she said reproachfully.

"I am talking of the average circumstances," said he—perhaps conscious that he was an exceptional one. "You will have all the fun that my cousins have, with nothing of their hard drill. While they are grinding away at Latin and French and German, you will have nothing but English literature to get up; and while they are hammering at fugues and sonatas, you will only have to practise your handwriting—and you can do that by writing to me. There will be no lawn-tennis as yet, of course; but you can play battledore-and-shuttlecock in the hall; and you will be expected to take part in entertainments for the instruction and amusement of the villagers—and won't that develop your self-confidence, Nanciebel!"

"I am sure Bristol must be a dreadful place to live in," said Nancy with a sigh.

"Why, it is one of the most beautiful towns in England!" he protested. "Of course you will be living a little way out in the country; but wait till I come to see you; I will take you into the town, and show you the College Green and the Whiteladies' Road, and Durdham Down, and Clifton Down, and the Suspension Bridge, and the steep banks of the Avon all hanging in foliage. Why, it is a beautiful neighborhood—not flat and tame like this, but with plenty of heights and cliffs and open spaces covered with hawthorn in the spring. Oh, I can tell you, Bristol is a most picturesque place!"

"What do I care about that?" said Nanciebel, as if in echo of "What's this dull town to me?" And then she continued, "Richard, I have got a little pocket almanac, and I am going to mark with red ink all the dates fixed for your coming to Bristol; and every night, before going to bed, I will score out the day that has passed, and say, 'There's another day of misery got over.'"

"And mind this, Nancy," he said, "though we have promised to send each other a letter only once a fortnight, that does not prevent you writing every day in the week, and keeping the sheets until the proper time has come. I'm sure I mean to do that; as I told you before, it will be a kind of diary; and you must tell me everything you are thinking, so that I may be certain I know exactly the truth. Oh, I don't say you may not find it a little lonely at first; you will be thinking of the pleasant evenings we have spent here, or the morning strolls out to the Weir Brake; but then, dearest, think of the necessity for the absence, and of all the greater happiness in store for us. There are very few engaged young people who have everything planned out so satisfactorily for them—friends approving—all the circumstances propitious— and what is a little waiting?"

"Ah, it's all very well for you, Richard," she said; "you are a man; and you are high-spirited and careless. But I shall feel so lonely—and— and there will be nobody to be good to me," confessed Nanciebel artlessly.

"You wait till I come down," said he, "and see if I don't make up for lost time."

And still more sad of heart was poor Nancy at the station on the following morning. She hardly spoke. Mr. Richard got her a *coupé*, and bribed the guard to keep it for her; she did not seem to care. Her elder brother was here to see her away, but he did not pay much attention to his sister; there were one or two acquaintances of his on the platform; and there was a parliamentary election somewhere in the neighborhood that seemed to interest them. As the time drew near, Nanciebel grew more and more dejected. She answered her lover's remarks in monosyllables chiefly, for her lips were tremulous, and she dared not trust herself. At last she had to get into the carriage. He kissed her; she took leave of him without a word—only pressing his hand; and the last he saw of her were her tear-filled eyes piteously and longingly regarding him. Then—long after the train had left the station—there was a flutter of a small white handkerchief from a carriage window; and that again disappeared at a curve in the line; Nanciebel was gone.

CHAPTER IV

NEW FRIENDS

For Mr. Richard, Stratford-on-Avon was an empty town after the departure of Nanciebel. He used to wander all round the neighborhood:

through the meadows, down by the river, or along to the Weir Brake; or again he would go away up to the top of Bardon Hill, and survey the wide landscape, identifying almost every feature of it with some recollection of his lost Nancy. Here was a lane in which she had made shy confession of her love, and sworn sweet vows of constancy until death; yonder was the highway in which, not a fortnight thereafter, they had had a furious quarrel; and still further along the point at which she had become suddenly penitent and had wept mild tears of contrition. He even went into the little shop in the High Street and begged Miss Kate Marlow to allow him to visit, in solitude and silence, the vacant little court-yard in which Nanciebel and he had conjured up so many fair dreams and visions of the future. Sister Kate was sympathetic and understood; she left him to himself, and gave him ample opportunity to become as miserable as he wished. But one afternoon Miss Kate had a more definite favor to bestow on him.

"I had a letter from Nancy this morning," she said, at the door of the shop. "I was wondering she did not write; but she said she waited until she got settled. Would you like to see it?"

"Oh, yes!" said he eagerly, "for she won't write to me until the end of next week. Of course, I am anxious to know how she takes to the place."

Therewith he followed Nanciebel's sister inside, and she went and got the letter. It was a long and elaborate composition, showing care as regards the handwriting; no doubt Nancy was already practising. But it was the contents that interested Mr. Richard—and surprised him. He expected that Nanciebel would be complaining of her sad fortune; pining for absent friends; recalling the pleasant hours she had passed with those she loved most; and wondering when her period of lone banishment was to be over. Nothing of the kind. In this letter Nancy seemed rather to be giving herself airs. Her sister was told of all the elegancies of life at the vicarage, even to the ringing of a dressing-bell before dinner; and was given to understand that Nancy was put in a position of perfect equality with the vicar's daughters, and even treated with consideration and respect by the lady-housekeeper—a somewhat awful person, as it appeared—who presided over the establishment. Mention was made of the Stanhope phaeton which had awaited her at the station. The garden of the vicarage communicated with that of Holiwell Court (Hon. G. Stapleton, brother of Lord De Vaux and Esk); and as the vicar's family had the free run of the place, Nancy, when the two young ladies were at their morning tasks, would sometimes wander into the hot-houses, where the Scotch head gardener told her the Latin names of the plants, and otherwise introduced her to the science of botany. And so Mr. Richard read on, momentarily expecting some reference to himself, but finding no such thing. He handed back those closely scribbled sheets, and thanked Miss Kate. Then he walked away home rather dispirited.

But a very different letter arrived at Woodend toward the close of the following week. There was no showing off or pride of place, but the outpourings and tender confidences of an innocent young soul, that might have melted a heart of stone. Oh, for the happy days, never to be recalled, which she had passed with her dear Richard in that beloved Stratford town! Here she was all alone, far, far from friends, with no one to cheer her or comfort her, with the future all grown dark and hopeless. The night brought wakeful hours of memory, and weeping over bygone happiness; the morning brought with it a renewed sense of isolation. A moan as of a dove deprived of its mate went all through this letter; and even while the young man prized and welcomed eagerly these artless confessions, his heart was stricken with sympathy and pity. Poor Nancy! Even the Stanhope phaeton, and the dressing-bell before dinner, and the Hon. Mr.

Stapleton's greenhouses, and the Scoto-Latin names of flowers, seemed not altogether to compensate. She still thought of her dear Richard, and of drowsy Stratford town, and the silent-winding Avon.

But the drowsiness of Warwickshire, so far as Mrs. Kingston and her son were concerned, was about to be broken in upon in a sudden and startling manner. Quite unexpectedly, without any warning, the news arrived that Richard's uncle out in China had at last accomplished the end he had long had in view—his retirement from the immediate direction of the firm of Kingston, Campbell & Co., of Shanghai, and that he and his step-daughter would almost immediately start for Europe. There were some further details in the letter. Uncle Alexander meant to set up house in London, after he had had time to look about; but, in the mean while, on his arrival, there would be a good deal of legal business to attend to, and he would take it as a kindness if his sister-in-law, for that brief period, would receive into her house his step-daughter Florence. Now, Mrs. Kingston had never even seen this young lady, who was a daughter, by a former husband, of Uncle Alexander's second and recently deceased wife. But the little widow never thought of evading this demand made upon her by her imperious and hot-tempered brother-in-law. It was not the aspect of this surprising intelligence which filled Mrs. Kingston's breast with concern.

"Richard," she said, going to her son with the letter in her hand, "your uncle Alexander and his daughter are coming to England; and he is going to bring her down here to stay with us a little while, until he gets some business over in London. And—and I suppose there will be a general talk over family affairs," continued the anxious mother, "and—and I suppose I shall have to tell him about Miss—about Nancy——"

Mr. Richard's face flushed quickly.

"I've said before, mother, that I expect Uncle Alexander to mind his own affairs," he remarked in ominous tones. "I am indebted to him in no way, and I don't mean to be. Did I ever ask him for any of his money? Who constituted him my guardian?"

"I am sure that your uncle Charles and I did what was right about—about Nancy," said the widow (who seemed always to have a little struggle in calling Miss Marlow by her Christian name), "but I know all the same that your uncle Alexander will be very angry—and you know how stormy and passionate he is——"

"Look here, mother," Mr. Richard said definitely, "I want you to understand this: I am not going to allow Uncle Alexander to worry you

about Nancy, or upon any other subject. If he
has anything to say, let him say it to me, and
he shall have his answer. But if I find him beginning to bully you, I shall show him the way to
the door. I suppose you may live all your life in
China and yet not have forgotten how to take a
hint."

Alas! when Uncle Alexander arrived at Woodend—accompanied by a tall, and handsome, and
bright-looking young lady, who appeared to take
possession of the whole house in a bewildering
sort of way—he was in no truculent mood. He
was a complete wreck, he declared. The long
voyage had shattered him; the rattling across
France had still further destroyed his nerves;
his consolation now was that he could lay his
bones to rest in his native land. It is true that
as Mr. Richard watched the performance of this
big, heavy, bilious-complexioned man at luncheon, he was of opinion that, for a moribund person, he possessed a remarkably brave appetite.
His harrowing description of the sensations he
suffered during the wakeful hours of night did
not interfere with his large consumption of steak
and kidney pie; and by the time that cheese and
celery were produced he had got through the best
part of a decanter of old Madeira. He had been
growing more and more silent, however, as the
repast proceeded; and when all rose from table,

he said he would retire to his own room and lie down for a while, as he found that a nap after lunch had a soothing effect on his nervous system.

And here were mother and son with this strange young lady left on their hands. But the strange young lady was in no wise disconcerted.

"Well, cousin," she said gayly, as she turned to Mr. Richard, "are you coming to show me over the curiosities of Stratford? I suppose I may call myself an Englishwoman; and an Englishwoman ought to know something of Stratford-on-Avon. How far is it in to the town?"

"A little over a couple of miles," said he; "but I will drive you in, if you like."

"Oh, thanks; that will be capital," said she. "You can tell me when the carriage is ready; I shall be in the drawing-room with Aunt Cecilia." And therewith she quite naturally and affectionately put her hand within the widow's arm and led her away with her.

In less than half an hour thereafter, Mr. Richard found himself seated next this light-hearted cousin of his, who had begged him to give her the reins. It was a pleasant afternoon; the snow had altogether disappeared from the country-side now; there were mild airs blowing, and a touch of sunlight here and there; a feeling of spring was abroad.

"I am awfully fond of driving," said she; "and driving through an English landscape in the spring-time—what can be better than that?"

"I'll have the pony-chaise brought round for you every morning if you like, Miss Kingston," he remarked.

"Miss Kingston!" she exclaimed, with an audacious smile. "Well, well! Why, my name is Floss; and I am your cousin; can't you put these two together, and give me a nicer name than Miss Kingston? I am going to call you Cousin Dick. You see," she continued, giving the reins a shake to wake up the old pony, "girls are subjected to such formalities and conventionalisms in ordinarily talking to gentlemen that, where there is a chance of a little familiarity, it is quite delightful. Cousin Dick sounds all right, doesn't it?"

"Y—yes," said he: he was thinking of poor little Nanciebel and her shy ways; and he was hoping that Kate Marlow might not see him and this dashing cousin of his if they had occasion to drive along the High Street.

When they got into Stratford, however, he put up the horse and trap at the stables belonging to a hotel where he was known; and thereafter they continued their peregrinations on foot. But first of all Cousin Floss paused at a milliner's window and looked in.

9

" Will you wait for me," said she, "or come in
and sit down? I'm going to buy some little
things for your mother, to break up the unrelieved
black of her mourning. Why, it isn't at all
called for; and it is the greater pity in her case,
for she is comparatively a young woman and very
nice-looking, and why should she wear nothing
but black? Of course, a widow will protest, and
may even think you cruel; but you have only to
talk a little common sense, and be firm; and
you'll see if I don't get something that will improve Aunt Cecilia's appearance."

She made her purchases, and sent them to the
hotel; then he took her along to New Place, and
showed her the site of Shakespeare's house; and
again he conducted her to the church, to the
shrine which so many pilgrims from all parts of
the world have visited. She betrayed the most
lively interest in everything he showed her, and
talked with an unfailing cheerfulness and frankness. At first, in fact, on setting out with this
newly found cousin, he had been rather taken
aback; her matter-of-fact audacity had somewhat
disconcerted him; but now he had grown familiar
with her fashion of addressing him just as if he
were her elder brother.

"Oh, my goodness!" she exclaimed, when he
showed her the Memorial Theatre—that fantastic
gew-gaw building set amid the placid river-side

scenery—"did ever any one see anything so
monstrous as that—so preposterous in itself, and
so out of keeping with the quiet, old-fashioned
town! Why, have you no public-spirited men
in England? Couldn't they raise a subscription
to buy that awful structure, and have it conveyed to the coast and hurled into the sea? How
do you expect Shakespeare's ghost to rest, with
a thing like that in the neighborhood?"

And then again, as they were driving home,
she said in her airy fashion:

"How do you spend the evenings, Cousin
Dick?"

"After dinner, you mean?" he said. "Oh,
well, the mater is always happy enough if she
has a volume of Tennyson, and I wander about
outside with a cigarette."

"You haven't a billiard-room?"

"No."

"Papa must see that there is a billiard-room in
the house he takes in London," continued Miss
Florence, with decision. "Gentlemen are too
valuable creatures of an evening to be allowed
to go away by themselves to smoke. And I'm
very fond of smoke."

"Perhaps you have tried a cigarette yourself?"
he asked, with a dash of impertinence.

"I?" she answered carelessly. "Oh, no. But
I can play billiards a little; and I don't care

how smoky the atmosphere is. By the way,
Cousin Dick, are you a good waltzer? "

"I don't know—middling, I suppose," was his
reply.

"That means you are a capital waltzer," she
said with much satisfaction, "and I'm delighted
to hear it. A cousin who is a good waltzer must
be simply invaluable; and when we get our
London house I shall rely on you to save me
from bad partners—an awful lot can be done by
skilful connivance. One of these evenings at
Woodend we'll clear the drawing-room and have
a turn, to see if our steps correspond; and, being
my cousin, you know, you won't be afraid to
catch hold of me—that is the worst of a bad
partner—a stranger—who seems to think you're
made of glass and will break if he touches you.
I like to feel that my partner has a good grip,
and knows where he is going."

When they reached home, they found that tea
had just been brought in to the widow's little
boudoir; and through the windows they could
see that Uncle Alexander was pacing up and down
the longest path in the garden outside—walking
with a quick, little, shuffling step, his head bent
forward, his arms swinging at his side.

"Shall I go and call your papa, Cousin Floss?"
said Mr. Richard—bravely tackling her newly
assumed style and title.

"Oh, no, no!" she cried. "He'll come in when he has done the regulation quantity. I have no doubt he has carefully measured out the forty-four yards; and forty times makes a mile, you know; but if you interrupt him he loses count, and has to begin the mile all over again—and that makes him cross, naturally. Poor papa! he used to be so put out on board ship—he never could get a stretch of the upper deck left undisturbed for him; as soon as he began, one of the officers would be sure to order up the Lascars to do something or other, or else some of the passengers would come and take possession with rope-quoits or shovel-board. I hope our London house will be in a square where papa will be able to get a measured space without being overlooked."

But when Uncle Alexander came in it was not to tea. He was groaning and complaining; he hardly knew which of his ailments demanded most immediate attention, whether it was the headache that lay across his brow like an iron clamp, or the heartburn that gnawed in his bosom like some internal rat, or the sickness and lassitude that seemed pulling him generally to the ground. Well, he attacked the heartburn first—with bicarbonate of soda. That proving of no avail, he had a thin slice of bread-and-butter thickly spread with cayenne pepper; and

having bolted that bolus, he washed it down
with a good stiff glass of brown brandy-and-
water. Whether the heartburn disappeared or
not, he seemed at least to recover a little from
the hopeless depression that had been hanging
over him; and he could now talk without a suc-
cession of melancholy sighs.

He was going up to town next morning, he
said. Would it be convenient for Aunt Cecilia
to have Florence remain with her for a week or
ten days, until he had seen to his business
affairs in London? The widow replied that she
would be most delighted—she had already cast
favoring eyes on this frank-spirited girl. Thereafter, again asked Uncle Alexander, would Aunt
Cecilia and Richard come up to town and be his
guests for a week or two at the private hotel he
was staying at in Arlington Street? Florence
wanted some one to show her about London; he
would be glad to have Aunt Cecilia's advice
about the choice of a house. The little widow
hesitated. The whirl of town life was not much
to her liking; she had grown accustomed to this
peaceful, secluded existence. But here Miss
Florence struck in, and declared that she would
only remain at Woodend on the understanding
that Aunt Cecilia and Cousin Dick should go to
London with her at the end of her stay; and that
settled the matter. The arrangement was finally

made, and Uncle Alexander returned to the garden to the measured forty-four yards that was to assist the action of the cayenne pepper and brandy.

So it came about that Florence Kingston was established at Woodend, where she speedily made herself felt as anything but a dull and depressing influence. The irresistible cheerfulness, the kindliness, the good humor of the girl acted as a kind of charm upon the solitary little widow, who thawed and warmed into smiles in the sunshine of this constant companionship. For it was not at all upon Mr. Richard that Cousin Floss bestowed her attention. Indeed, she treated that young man in somewhat of a cavalier spirit; it was the gentle mother whom she petted, and teased, and spoiled, and laughed at, all at once.

"I declare, Richard," said the widow, on one occasion when Cousin Floss had just left the room, "when that girl goes out, it is just as if a hurricane had passed by—leaving a sudden calm behind it."

"And yet you don't seem to dislike her, mater," he observed.

"Dislike her? No. Sometimes I think I am getting too fond of her," the widow said, with a sigh; perhaps she was thinking of what might have been.

Then came the evening on which the great

waltzing experiment was to be tried. As well
as they could they cleared the tables and chairs
from the larger drawing-room; and Mrs. Kingston was asked to officiate at the piano. How
long was it since the widow had played a waltz,
or any other species of musical composition, for
the matter of that? Nevertheless, she could refuse this headstrong girl nothing; so presently
she was strumming away at some fine old-fashioned tune, while the young people were gliding
round the cleared space to the tinkle-tankle of
the venerable instrument. When they stopped,
Miss Florence was good enough to say:

"You do very well, Cousin Dick. Oh, yes;
you and I will have a little practice every evening, and we'll get into each other's ways perfectly. I like your reversing; you're not afraid
to catch hold. And then I shall rely on you in
London, mind. Whenever I want to get rid of
a bore or a bad dancer I shall claim you. You
must be at my beck and call. It's wonderful
what tricks you can play with a programme when
you have an accomplice; and when the accomplice is your cousin, it's all right, don't you
see?"

But the opportunities for bringing this dark
conspiracy into operation were as yet afar off;
for when Mrs. Kingston and Mr. Richard eventually went up to London with Cousin Floss, the

whole party found themselves in a private hotel, Uncle Alexander not yet having provided himself with a house. And meanwhile, as the retired China merchant was still being called upon to go into the city on business matters, the introducing of Miss Florence to the ways and customs of the town, and to its outward features as well, fell upon these two Warwickshire folk, who were almost as much strangers as herself. That, however, did not matter much to Mr. Richard, who had the arrangement of their little excursions, and rather liked going about with this pretty and vivacious cousin. The barouche which Uncle Alexander had hired he seldom was allowed to make use of; it was in almost constant requisition for the three sight-seers. Miss Florence was, of course, taken to the Tower. The British Museum did not occupy much of her time; but a students' day in the National Gallery interested her keenly. She heard part of a debate in the House of Commons, and had tea in the tea-room. She hunted out the neighborhoods that had grown familiar to her in her favorite novels; was that, then, the actual building in which poor Angelica had sat and stitched, and watered her bread with tears, and given her lover up for dead—the lover who was pining in a Spanish prison far away, and even hoping to regain his native land? Other buildings also, whose names she had heard of, she was taken to visit—the Trafalgar at Greenwich, the Star and Garter at Richmond, and so forth; and most frankly did she enjoy the little festivities that accompanied these wanderings. Then there were concerts and theatres for an occasional afternoon or evening; hardly a day seemed long enough. The widow grew quite cheerful through her constant association with this bright and bold young life that was showing all its pleasantest characteristics in these varied scenes; Mr. Richard had never seen her look so well or so happy; and she was content (if with a smile of doleful resignation) to wear whatever Miss Florence imperiously insisted on her wearing. Uncle Alexander, it may be observed, remained apart from these gayeties. For one thing, his business arrangements did not go forward quite as smoothly as he had expected; for another, the state of his health called for a constant care. He was his own physician. He had found that ordinary doctors were rude persons, who were not ashamed to hint that he ought to eat and drink less and take more exercise. He knew that his many ailments arose from far more recondite causes, and demanded the most studious treatment. These continuous escapades on the part of his daughter and her two relatives were not for him. How could he be expected to go and breathe the polluted air of a theatre, when he had to be in his own room, looking every ten minutes at his tongue in a mirror? But he was glad to think that Floss had youth and health and spirits to enjoy all that mad gadding about; and he hoped that his sister-in-law and her son would prolong their stay in London as long as they conveniently could.

Amid all this whirl of amusement and enjoyment Mr. Richard suddenly remembered that the day appointed for his first visit to Bristol was drawing near; and perhaps he had an uneasy consciousness that he had been somewhat neglectful of poor little Nanciebel. He had not written to her literally every morning—for life in London was a desperately busy thing; and sometimes his budget of news for the week was a somewhat perfunctory affair. However, that would all be put right now. Letter-writing was an ineffective thing at the best. When he was once more face to face with his sweetheart—her tender eyes looking into his—she would know that he had been true to her in absence. And would they not both congratulate each other that the first two months of that cruel separation were now over?

When Cousin Floss heard that he was going down to Bristol on the following Monday she was indignant.

"What for?" she demanded in her straight-forward way.

"I have an appointment—that I must keep," said he.

"Why, it is Monday night we were going to see 'The Winter's Tale' at the Lyceum—papa got the box a fortnight ago. And you know your mother and I just hate going anywhere by ourselves. How far away is Bristol? Can't you come back in time to take us to the theatre?"

Well, the truth is he had intended staying the night at Holiwell Vicarage, in order to have a long evening with Nanciebel; but then, on the other hand, both his mother and cousin looked so naturally to him for escort and guidance that he was almost bound to return and take them to the Lyceum as they wished. There was an afternoon train leaving Bristol which would bring him to Paddington at 6:30; that would just give him time to get to the hotel, snatch a bit of dinner, and dress. So he told Cousin Floss that she should not be balked of "The Winter's Tale" on his account.

He left London on the Monday morning by the 9 o'clock express, and reached Bristol at 12. During the journey down he had been possessed not so much with joy at the prospect of meeting Nanciebel as with a half-confessed fear that she might begin to cross-examine him, and be petu-

lant, and cause trouble. He was conscious that
the sorrow of separation had not fallen equally
on him and her—he had had distractions, about
which the less said the better. And when, on
arriving at Holiwell Vicarage, and being ushered
into the drawing-room, he found that along with
Nanciebel there were his two cousins and also
the governess, perhaps he was somewhat relieved. Yet Nanciebel looked so gentle!—and
so pleased at his coming, too. She regarded him
covertly with her dark, soft eyes; and a man-
tling blush suffused her cheek when he made bold
to address a word or two to her direct. "Mr.
Kingston," she called him before the vicar's
daughters and the governess. There was something odd and unexpected about the way she
wore her hair now—and about her dress, too—
that did not escape his notice; she seemed to
have undergone some kind of transformation,
though he could not define it exactly; she was
hardly the same Nanciebel who used to walk up
and down the little court-yard with him, crisp
snow underfoot and shining and throbbing stars
overhead.

Luncheon-bell rang and the vicar appeared at
the same time; in a minute or two they were all
assembled at table in the dining-room. And
Uncle Charles was full of questions about his
brother-in-law Alexander and his plans, and also

about his niece, or quasi-niece, Florence, whom he had never seen. On this latter point Mr. Richard was frankly talkative, not to say effusive; and Nanciebel, on the other side of the table, listened in silence. A stranger might have fancied that she and this handsome young man had now met for the first time; and that the quiet little country girl was rather impressed by his stories of the fine doings in London town.

After luncheon, the various members of the small household discreetly went their several ways, leaving Mr. Richard and his sweetheart by themselves. But still there were servants about, so Nanciebel said shyly:

"Will you come into the garden, Richard?"

"Anywhere you like, Nancy," he answered; and he followed her through the open French window and down the wide stone steps. It was a large, old-fashioned garden; and there were walls of yew intersecting it.

"I am so glad to see you again, Richard," she said, with downcast eyes (she did not dare to take his arm, for there might be a spectator at one or other of the windows).

"And I am glad to find you looking so well," said he. "I was sure you would find my uncle and my cousins as kind as you could wish. I saw that from the first, in your letters, though you weren't quite—quite as—as outspoken as you might have been."

"Were you disappointed, Richard?" she said humbly. "But you don't know, dear, how lonely I have been since I came here! Yes, they are very kind; but kindness isn't everything," she continued, with a bit of a sigh. "When I think of those days at Stratford—ah, that was different!"

"Yes, I know, Nanciebel," he said. "But you can't expect everything. I know you are very warm-hearted; and you like to have people say nice things to you, and be good to you, and pet you. But that can't be always and everywhere; and I don't think you are so badly off."

"It's all very well for you to say so," said Nanciebel, with some rebellious spirit, "when you are having every possible enjoyment and amusement along with that cousin of yours. Of course *you* don't feel dull. Of course *you* don't feel lonely."

"Well," said he sharply, "I don't pine and fret if there is no one by to say pretty things and give me caresses."

"I dare say she would if you asked her," said Nanciebel, with a toss of her head.

He drew in his breath—but stopped ere any word of anger could escape. No, he had not come down here to quarrel with Nancy. And

after all might there not be some little justifica-
tion? Had he quite realized her loneliness?
Had he honestly contrasted it with the gay time
he had been spending in London?

"We needn't fall out, Nanciebel," said he
slowly. "I have only a short time to stay."

"A short time to stay?" she repeated. "Why,
when are you going back?"

"By the 3:42," he made answer.

There was a momentary silence.

"Richard," said she, "here is the time come
we have been looking forward to so long—at
least that I have been looking forward to; and
you take advantage of it to the extent of a couple
of hours. Are you sure it wasn't a mere sense
of duty that brought you here at all? Perhaps
you didn't want to come?"

"Perhaps I didn't want to come!" he said impatiently. And then he controlled himself, and
said in quite an altered tone:

"Oh, stuff and nonsense, Nanciebel! Why
will you insist on quarrelling, you little quick-
tempered, warm-hearted stupid! Come, kiss and
be friends."

They were at the moment passing through an
arched opening cut in the thick wall of yew; and
she obediently paused, and did as she was bid.
The reconciliation was complete. She took him
to see Mr. Stapleton's greenhouses, and intro-

duced him to the head gardener—a young Scotchman of eight-and-twenty or so, who, as she afterward informed him, was prodigiously clever, had attended classes at Glasgow University, though he was then quite poor, and was now so recognized a *master* of his art that he had been offered the equivalent of his present situation at Beever Towers, the seat of the Duke of Grandon. She led him round to show him the caged eagles, and the white peacocks, and what-not; indeed, she seemed just as much at home here at Holiwell Court as at the adjoining vicarage. Then she pointed out that if he must really go by the 3:42 train, it was about time for him to return indoors.

Both his cousins and Nanciebel drove with him in to the town to see him off. The parting between him and Nancy was necessarily not effusive—for Gertrude and Laura were looking on, and they were merry and talkative girls who would hardly leave him alone for a second. Nor were there tears in Nanciebel's eyes as the train moved away from the station and as she waved her handkerchief to him in final adieu. In fact, this leave-taking was far different from that which had occurred when Nanciebel bade goodby to Stratford; but was it not better that it should be so, he asked himself, as he sat alone in the carriage, and was being rapidly whirled away

toward London? Nancy seemed more satisfied
with this separation now—if at times she complained that there was no one to be good to her.
And meanwhile—meanwhile he would get to
Arlington Street in time to slip into evening
dress and take his mother and Cousin Floss to
the Lyceum.

———

CHAPTER V

FLIGHT

ON that same afternoon Uncle Alexander came
home from the city; and finding his step-daughter and Mrs. Kingston together, he without any
apology—for rudeness is a prerogative of dys-
pepsia—ordered Miss Florence to go to her own
room; he had something particular to say to Aunt
Cecilia. He sat down by the fire, and stared into
the coals; he seemed more sallow and sluggish
than ever; and when he spoke it was in slow and
mournful tones.

"I do not know how long I am for this world,
Cecilia," he observed. "Every day I become
more depressed. I cannot shake it off—I have
lost hope—I hardly care how soon the end may
be."

"Perhaps London does not agree with you," the widow said, with gentle sympathy. "Why should you not try travelling, Uncle Alexander— on the Continent?"

"Try travelling!" he exclaimed, in sudden and angry impatience. "God bless my soul, haven't I tried travelling sufficiently? Haven't I just come home from China? Would you like me to go back to Shanghai for a change? I wish you would listen, and not interrupt with fatuities; how long do I know I may be able to make my wishes known?" And then he continued in more business-like tones: "Now, this is what I want to say—that in view of what may happen to me at any time, I wish to make the best provision I can for those I leave behind—those I am most interested in. Florence has the first claim, of course, though she is not of my blood. Richard, on the other hand, is of my own kith and kin. Very well; when I have made certain smaller bequests, the bulk of my property will remain to be divided as between these two."

"It is so generous of you, Uncle Alexander!" the widow broke in. "But surely there is no occasion for you to talk like that! Surely not! Why, I should call you an exceptionally strong man."

"I wish you to listen, if you please, Cecilia," observed the dyspeptic, with a dignity natural to

one who was speaking of his own nearly
approaching end. "I was going to say that there
might be some difficulty in deciding what rela-
tive portion should be assigned to either of these
two; but that what has been happening of late
seems to point to an easy way out of the difficulty. You must have noticed how capitally
these two get on together—how fond they seem
of each other's society. Ah, well," he continued, with a heavy sigh, "youth is a fine thing,
and health, and absence from care: let them
enjoy them while they can!"

But sudden consternation filled the heart of
the little widow; she knew what he meant; and
she found herself on the brink of a confession
which she had put off from day to day, vainly
hoping that the need of it would not arise.

"Oh, yes, Uncle Alexander," she observed,
rather breathlessly. "I am glad to see them
such good friends. It is but right they should
be so—almost of an age—and cousins—it is only
to be expected——"

"I should like to see them married before I
go," continued the invalid absently. "Or if that
is denied me, I should like to know that that settlement of their lives was to take place, and I
could make provision for them in proper form."

"Uncle Alexander," said the widow, with her
trembling fingers nervously clasped together,

"it is most kind and generous of you to have such intentions in view. But—but I think—I must explain—as regards Richard, what you propose is impossible. I have said that I am delighted to see him and his cousin on such friendly terms—but—but that is all there is between them."

"Oh, yes, I understand," Uncle Alexander said impatiently. "I understand. Of course nothing has been declared between them. That is quite right. There has not been a sufficient length of time. But we, who are outsiders and spectators, can see clearly enough what will happen."

"O Uncle Alexander," she exclaimed in her distress, "it can never happen."

He stared at her.

"What do you mean, Cecilia?" he demanded.

"Richard is—is already engaged to be married," she blurted out.

There was no explosion of wrath; he only continued to stare at her as if she were an imbecile, whose utterances were wholly unintelligible.

"But—but—what was that?—impossible?— what did you say? Richard engaged to be married?" he repeated, with non-understanding eyes.

The ordeal had to be faced. She began, and with piteous excuses for not having made the revelation before, she told him the whole story.

Uncle Alexander sat and listened, dumfounded beyond the power of speech. A sort of despair and resignation overwhelmed him. And when she had finished he could only ejaculate:

"Well, well, if any human being ever heard of such a gigantic piece of tomfoolery!"

But presently he said, with a blaze of anger:

"Why, don't you know that every young idiot gets into a scrape like that, and that it is the business of his relatives—unless they're fools—unless they're fools—to get him out of it? Don't you know it's as common as shelling peas? You talk to me as if it was a piece of romantic sentiment—Miller's Daughter be hanged!—and that the young idiot should rather be praised for holding to the girl! I tell you it happens every day —and will happen every day as long as idle lads are allowed to dawdle about, and there are shop-girls and milliner-girls and barmaids to make eyes at them. And instead of getting him out of the scrape, you treat the whole thing as serious! Gracious heavens! But I must put this matter right. What's the girl's name? How much does she want? What size of a check has she got in her eye?"

Mrs. Kingston flushed a little.

"I wish you to understand, Uncle Alexander," said she with unusual firmness, "that the girl is a good and honest girl, and not a designing adventuress at all—that I am convinced of; and I do not see why she should be insulted simply because of her station in life—which is perfectly respectable and honorable, if it comes to that."

"Stuff and fiddlesticks!" cried Uncle Alexander. Indeed, this sharp crisis in the family affairs seemed to have suddenly banished all that languor and depression which, according to his account, were dragging him down to the tomb. "You're too fond of romance and poetry, Cecilia; and that's the fact. You want a little common sense to come in to put matters straight. Where is this girl?"

"At Holiwell Vicarage," Mrs. Kingston answered. "Uncle Charles is taking charge of her for the present."

The China merchant stared at her again.

"No," said he solemnly; "no, Cecilia, you cannot mean that there are three such fools in the family! Two I could have borne with—but three! Uncle Charles as well!—upon my soul, it's beyond belief!"

But the meanest worm will turn.

"I wish to say this once for all, Uncle Alexander," observed the little widow, with very considerable dignity, "that I hope you will not speak to Richard as you have done to me this afternoon. His temper is not so much under control as mine; he would probably answer you in your own language. Propose to him that the girl he is engaged to should be offered a sum of money, and I know one certain consequence—he would never darken your door again, nor would you or yours ever enter our house. As for my share in this matter, I am not ashamed of it. I have done what I thought was right. Richard's word is pledged to a good and honorable girl; and if he is my son he will not disgrace himself —I say, disgrace himself—by seeking to break that bond, whatever pecuniary and mercenary inducements may be placed before him."

She rose as if to leave the room.

"Cecilia!" he said, to stay her.

"No," she made answer, "let that be the last word. I wish for peace between the two families. There will be no peace—there will be a lasting rupture and estrangement if you propose that Richard should do anything dishonorable, merely because you have had certain plans in view. I do not say that in other circumstances I might not have wished as you wish; but as matters stand I hope my son will act as becomes the name he bears. And another thing, Uncle Alexander: neither he nor Florence need know that a word has passed between us on the sub-ject. They are very good friends and nothing more; let them remain such—if you choose it to be so. If not, then my boy and I can return to

Woodend at once, and we shall not trouble you again."

She did not wait for an answer. She forthwith quitted the room, leaving Uncle Alexander entirely out-talked and astonished. He had not anticipated this display of firmness—this bold upstanding of what he considered idiotic sentiment against the rude and doughty onslaughts of common sense. And when he began to consider matters, he had to confess that perhaps he had been a little premature. That this shop-girl could be bought off he was convinced; but he had erred in making the proposition too suddenly to the widow. Then, again, he would have a better right to interfere when the relationship between Richard and Florence had become developed—in the obvious and proper direction, of course. What! Richard marry a penniless little seamstress in Stratford-on-Avon— a shy, speechless nonentity, as the widow had half admitted—when here was his bright and fascinating cousin, an heiress, gifted with every qualification, a fit helpmeet, one who would do him honor in society? Uncle Alexander, seated by the slumbering fire, was so intent upon these various schemes and considerations that he forgot he had allowed a whole hour to elapse since he had examined his tongue in the mirror—and during that hour he had kept his daughter Flor-

ence a prisoner upstairs; and when eventually he
went away to his own room, to seek safety and consolation in his medicine chest, he was still of
opinion that the widow's quixotic ideas of duty
and her son's chivalrous resolves with regard to
that wretched little milliner-girl—was she a milliner-girl? he had forgotten—would in time be
overcome.   For great is the power of common
sense.

Accordingly, Uncle Alexander did not return
to this project; and as the widow heard no more
of it, she, in turn, was silent, so that the two
cousins were thrown into association just as here-
tofore, ignorant of the dark schemes and designs
which had been foreshadowed with regard to
their future.   And the better to secure his sinister end, Uncle Alexander declared that for the
present he was going to abandon his intention
of taking and fitting out a London house: it was
too much trouble.   He did not know but that, if
his health continued to grow worse, he and Florence might not go away to one of the German
baths, so that he might try a course of the waters.   In the mean time he discovered a furnished
residence in Melbury Road which would serve
their needs.   And could not the widow postpone
her return to Woodend for a while, so as to initi-
ate Florence into her duties as house-mistress?
When Florence preferred the same request—or

rather imperiously insisted, with all kinds of
direful threats and cunning coaxings—Mrs.
Kingston yielded; she could refuse nothing to
this wild-spirited Cousin Floss.

It was hardly fair to put any young man's constancy to such a perilous test; but Mr. Richard,
even while giving himself up to the full enjoyment of the society of this charming cousin,
could always still his conscience and reassure
himself by writing a more than usually affectionate letter to Nanciebel. And why should he
send a too minute account of their gay doings
when he knew that that would only wound the
poor faithful heart? Nancy had already betrayed a suspicious curiosity about the Florence
whom he briefly mentioned from time to time,
and had even begun to demand explanations.

"Why, you see, Nanciebel," he wrote in reply,
"my uncle and his step-daughter know very few
people in London as yet; and as he is a good deal
in the city, the time would hang very heavily on
her hands if the mater did not take her about a
little. Then, of course, I have to accompany
these two. I could not let them wander about
London all by themselves; but do you think it
is any pleasure to *me* to go to the Tower or to
the South Kensington Museum? And then,
again, when any people send them an invitation,
the mater and I are sure to be included, as it is

known we are staying with them; and it is but natural that in a strange house, if there is any dancing or anything going on, Florence should count upon me, as her cousin. I don't see how you can object; but you have such a tendency to magnify trifles! When I express regret over our engagement, or ask you to release me, then you will have a right to complain; but in the mean time you needn't grumble about nothing."

Nanciebel's answer to this was written in a dozen different moods: by turns she was indignant, rebellious, petulant, and piteously imploring.

"What is the use of keeping me here?" she asked. "What is the use of it? Did you see any difference in me when you came down that day —except in the dressing of my hair? And did you think it an improvement—an improvement worth all this loneliness and misery? *Once* you would have said that my hair could not be improved; *once* you would have declared it was the prettiest in the world; but that was long ago— that was before your cousin Florence came to England. I know you will be in a rage because I talk of misery; and you will accuse me of ingratitude, and ask what more I want. Well, I needn't attempt to tell you, for you wouldn't understand; but I can remember the time when you were more in sympathy with my feelings, and when there was no fear of my being misunderstood. *Once* you would not have left me to pine like this; you would not have yielded to relatives; you were ready to do *anything* for my sake. But I suppose it's the way of the world; and *you*, of course, can't regret an absence that brings you so much—and such charming—consolation.

"I have written—I only know that I just hate being alone. Oh, for the happy mornings and afternoons when I could sit and listen at every footstep on the pavement outside, and think that any moment my Richard might come in! You did not want me improved *then*. I suppose you never think now of the Bideford Road, and the lane leading down to Shottery, and the meadows. It seems a long time ago now to poor me. I sit and think that never, never again there will be the long, still, beautiful evenings, and us two on the banks of the Avon, seated beneath the bushes, and watching the boys fishing on the other side, under the Weir Brake. Those were happy, happy days! Will they ever come again, Richard, dear? Do say something kind to me when you write—I don't mean the kindness I get from the vicar and his daughters, but *real* kindness, for I am so lonely and miserable!"

Now this appeal, couched in its artless language, made Mr. Richard not a little remorseful;

and his contrition suddenly assumed the shape
of a resolve to go to Cousin Floss and tell her all
about his engagement to Nanciebel. He did not
stay to ask why that should be considered as
making amends to Nancy; he only felt that he
was somehow called upon to tell the whole truth;
then Florence could think of him as she pleased.
Was it not due to poor Nanciebel? Why should
she be ignored amid all these gayeties and distractions? She had her rights. And she had
not been too exacting—her last letter had been
piteous rather than petulant and quarrelsome.

But this proved to be a terrible business. He
chose an opportunity when Cousin Floss had gone
out into the garden to have a look at the spring
blossoms or perchance to survey, with feminine
curiosity, the backs of the artists' houses, across
the low brick wall. When he overtook her, she
was apparently busy with snowdrops and prim-
roses and daffodils; and she was so good-natured
as to pick for him a purple crocus and even to
fix it into the lapel of his coat. How could he
refuse this simple kindness?—he was not a boor.
Nevertheless, in about twenty minutes or so,
he and she and the little widow were to set out
for the private view of a certain picture-gallery,
where they would most likely meet such people
as they knew; and he would be wearing Cousin
Floss' flower in his buttonhole. Was he going

about with her, then, under false pretences? The confession had become all the more imperative.

But how was he to begin?

"Cousin," said he with a most unusual hesitation—for, under her skilful tuition, he had come to address her in the most frank and open and unconventional manner—"did my mother ever speak to you—about—about—a Miss Marlow?"

She noticed his embarrassment instantly.

"Why, no!" she said, in some surprise. "Miss Marlow? No—I don't think I ever heard the name. Who is she?"

How could he explain? He wished that Cousin Floss had not such clear eyes, and a mouth so ready to smile.

"At present," he went on in rather a stammering fashion, "she—she is living with my uncle Charles at Bristol—at the vicarage, near Bristol."

Cousin Floss laughed.

"The governess?" she said.

"No—no—but I have something to tell you about her. I think I ought to tell you—for sooner or later you will hear of it," he continued —and he was blushing like a school-girl, because Cousin Floss was evidently amused by his timidity. "I thought the mater would have told you——"

All of a sudden Miss Florence put her hand

within his arm in the most friendly way, and thereby intimated that she wished him to pace up and down the garden path with her.

"Cousin Dick!" she protested, "I won't hear a word! I know what you've got to tell me— and I can see how it vexes you—but I will spare you the confession. Oh, don't I know what dreadful flirts young men are—don't I know!— but they can't help it, the poor dears, and I am always ready to forgive them—because—because —well, because there are sometimes girls wicked enough to lead them on, and pretend they enjoy it, too! Cousin Dick, why should you tell me? —do you think it would be news?"

"Oh, but you're quite mistaken, Florence!" he exclaimed. "Quite mistaken! I assure you she is not the kind of girl to amuse herself in that way at all——"

"Oh, a simple innocent, is she?" said Cousin Floss, with another little bit of a laugh. "Yes, they sometimes look like that—sometimes it is part of the game—with the clever ones——"

"Oh, but really——"

"Oh, but really," she repeated, with the most obvious good-nature, "I won't hear another word! I won't, indeed, Cousin Dick! Do you think I don't understand? You see, my dear cousin, a girl who has lived a good part of her life in India, and a still longer time in China, and knows what a voyage in a P. and O. ship is like—well, she isn't quite a baby, you know—not *quite* a baby—and if you were to begin with your confessions, I might have to begin with mine; and wouldn't that be mutually awkward? I wish you had seen a young aide-de-camp, a Captain Webster, who came on board, this last trip, at Aden, and remained with us as far as Suez. He was a *dear*—and that's a fact; but papa didn't seem to see much in him—papas never do see anything in young men who have a pretty mustache but no income to speak of. So, you understand, cousin, I might have a story or two to tell as well as you; and I shouldn't like it, for blushing doesn't become me; besides, it is far safer and nicer for every one to let bygones be bygones. No, you needn't interrupt, Cousin Dick; I won't hear another word from you—not a word; we will both let bygones be bygones; I tell you, it's safer."

And as Mrs. Kingston appeared at this moment at the French window, and called to them, what could he do? He gave up the hope of explaining to his cousin. He went to the private view, wearing the flower she had given him. And if any one drew inferences from his being constantly seen with her—well, how could he help that?

In due course of time the visit of Mrs. King-

10*

ston and her son to their London relatives came
to an end; and they returned to their Warwickshire home. But they very soon discovered that
a singular change had come over the house.
Woodend was solitary as they had never known
it to be in former days. There was something
wanting in these silent rooms: a voice, with clear
laughter ringing in its tones, and joy, and audacity, was now heard no more in the hall; the
garden, though all the splendors of the spring
were beginning to declare themselves in plot,
and bed, and border, seemed empty now.

"I could not have believed I should have
missed her so much," the widow said sadly.

And as for Mr. Richard, he was ill at ease.
His thoughts, which he knew should have been
turned toward Bristol, went in quite another
direction, and would hover, in spite of himself,
about Kensington and the neighborhood of Hol-
land Park. Poor Nanciebel's fortnightly letters
to himself were not looked for half so eagerly
as Cousin Floss' hasty scrawls sent down to her
dear aunt Cecilia; and Mr. Richard would lie in
wait for these, and, whenever he found one on
the hall-table, he would at once carry it to his
mother, with the seemingly careless question,
"What has Florence to say now, mater?" For,
indeed, Cousin Floss seemed to find a great many
things to say to the widow. She was continually

writing on some kind of excuse; and she invariably wound up with pretty and affectionate speeches, and hopes of a speedy reunion. Cousin Floss did not write to Mr. Richard, of course—that was too much to expect; but in one way or another his name generally came to be mentioned; and sometimes there were tantalizing and even impertinent messages for him.

"Who is this Captain Webster, Richard, dear?" the widow asked on one occasion.

Mr. Richard blushed angrily.

"Oh, he's some young idiot—aide-de-camp to a colonial governor or something of that kind."

"But why should Florence send you this message about him?" Mrs. Kingston asked again.

"Oh, well," said he, with a fine air of assumed indifference, "Florence told me something about him before—he was on board the steamer they came home in—and as he left the ship at Gibraltar, I suppose she was surprised when she found him turn up in London."

Meanwhile the continual unrest and downheartedness that had characterized his manner ever since their return to Woodend had not escaped the anxious mother's eyes; and one evening she made bold to speak of it.

"Well, mater," said he, "I don't know what it is, except that I feel I am in a wrong position altogether. I am tired of doing nothing. I want to go away. Look at Nancy; the separation that was agreed upon tells more hardly on her than on me, for she is kept apart from her friends and relatives, while I live on just as before. It's hardly fair. I think I should go away from England for a time—for a considerable time—until, indeed, this period of separation ends, and then I could come back and marry Nancy, and everything would be settled and right. I am sure, if once the wedding took place, all would be well."

"I suppose," said the widow absently, "that my selfishness must be punished in the end. It was I who have kept you in idleness, Richard, and now you fret, and want to go. I should have thought you could have found some way of passing the few months that must elapse now before the settlement you speak of. And if you find the house so dull—well, I had not intended to tell you—it was a little surprise we had arranged—but Florence is coming down to stay with us for a while."

"Is Florence coming down here?" he asked slowly, and with a strange expression of face.

Something peculiar in his tone struck her. She looked up as she said:

"Yes. It was to be a little surprise for you——"

"Mother," he said hastily, "I will not be in

this house when Florence comes. You must make some excuse for me. I will go abroad; or I will go down to Bristol and live in the town, and only see Nancy from time to time But I—I don't want to be here when Florence comes."

The truth flashed upon her in an instant; but, amid all her alarm and bewilderment, she had the courage to say in a low voice:

"You are right, Richard. If it is as I suspect —ah, well, there is no use thinking now of what might have been—you must none the less do what is right. It was thoughtless of me to ask Florence to come down again; but how could any one help loving her?—she is such a dear girl, so bright and clever and good-tempered; but you, Richard, your honor is at stake. Of course you have said nothing to her? "

"To Florence?—certainly not, mother. How could I? But there is not another word to be said. You must make some excuse for me to Florence; and I must go."

No, there was no use saying anything further; but the widow could not help adding, almost in an undertone, and wistfully:

"If things could only have been different, Richard! I cannot help thinking that Florence —well, she has always seemed so much interested in you—and she would always talk so much about you, when she and I were alone together;

and you yourself see how you are never out of
her letters—ah, well, it is no use thinking of
what is impossible; but if you had been free,
and if you had gone to your cousin, I don't think
you need have feared her answer——"

He turned very pale.

"Don't say that—you have no right to say
that, mother!"

"It is but a guess on my part," she said sadly.
"But I can imagine what her answer would
have been. And then to think of her in this
house — as my daughter and companion — so
cheerful and self-reliant—so merry and good-
humored——"

"Mother," said he almost reproachfully, "you
seem to forget!"

"No, I don't forget," she answered with resignation. "I was thinking of what might have
been; but I don't forget. And you are doing
right, Richard. I will make excuses to Florence for you, whether you go abroad or down to
Bristol. I suppose she will not suspect—no, she
cannot suspect, if you have said nothing to her."

Nor was this the only act of renunciation on
Mr. Richard's part. Just at this time he had to
go up to London for a few days to transact some
business with his mother's lawyers; but he did
not apprise his uncle and cousin of his coming to
town, nor did he once call at the house in Mel-

bury Road. It is true that, during these few
days, he found his way a number of times to
that neighborhood, and on more than one occasion he caught a glimpse of Cousin Floss, as she
drove up in the barouche, or came out walking
with her maid. He knew he had no right to do
this thing; but he regarded it as a sort of bidding good-by to a broken fancy, an impossible
dream. To whom could it do any harm?
Cousin Floss could know nothing of it—he stu-
diously kept himself concealed. If this unspoken
farewell was unduly prolonged (for he remained
in London some days longer than was necessary
for the lawyers) it was himself who was being
lacerated by its pain. It did not matter to
Nancy; marriage would condone everything;
she had no part or concern in these fantasies of
the hour, that would soon be forgotten among
the actualities of life.

By the time Cousin Floss' visit drew near,
Mr. Richard had made all his preparations. He
was going down to Bristol. He argued with
himself that being constantly in the same neighborhood with Nanciebel would keep alive in his
recollection what was due to her; and, moreover,
he considered that in the circumstances he might
fairly ask for some modification of the arrangements that had been arrived at in family conclave
with regard to his visits. Might he not see

Nanciebel once a week, or perhaps even twice a week—for a single hour? Both he and she had hitherto loyally obeyed the conditions that had been imposed; might not these be relaxed a little now? It was not as a punishment, but as a test, that this separation had been agreed upon; and here were the two of them, after the lapse of a considerable time, of the same mind. Mr. Richard endeavored to extract courage and hope for the future from these wise and virtuous reflections; but it was with rather a heavy heart that he drove away to the station, on the day previous to Cousin Floss' arrival.

Cousin Floss, when she stepped out of the pony-chaise on the following afternoon, and found the widow awaiting her in the porch, was in the highest spirits, and her always bright enough eyes fairly shone with gladness.

"Do you know, Aunt Cecilia," said she as she hugged and kissed the little woman, "it is just like getting home again to see your dear face once more. When I saw Thomas and the pony and the carriage at the station, I said to myself, 'Ah, now you will soon be among old friends!'"

"Come away in, dear," said the widow quite as affectionately, and she took the girl by the arm and led her into the house. "I declare it does my heart good to hear your voice again."

"And papa is so sorry he couldn't come with

me this time," continued this blithe young damsel—who looked all round the drawing-room as if expecting to see some one—"but the fact is, he has found himself a good deal better of late, and he thinks it is because the Kensington neighborhood suits him, and he likes the house. The garden is just forty yards long; so twenty-two times up and down makes an easily-measured half-mile; and he can get his regulation quantity done every day without being overlooked by anybody. I think he will keep that house. He hasn't been looking about for any other. But—but—Aunt Cecilia," continued Miss Florence, again glancing back into the hall, "where is Cousin Dick?"

Only for the moment did the widow seem a little embarrassed.

"He has had to go away, dear," she said, striving to appear quite placid and unconcerned. "He was so very sorry—I was to tell you how sorry he was. Nothing but the most absolute necessity compelled him—you may be sure of that."

"He has gone away?" said Cousin Floss, in return, with a kind of puzzled, uncertain look. "Where has he gone, Aunt Cecilia?"

"To Bristol, dear," answered the widow.

"Oh, to Bristol!" repeated the young lady slowly. "That is where his uncle lives—his uncle Charles—isn't it?"

And when Mr. Richard's mother signified assent, the young lady said no more. She seemed a trifle thoughtful as she went away to her own room to look to her things; but when she appeared at dinner she was as cheerful as ever; and the widow, with affectionate eyes and many a kindly speech, showed how she rejoiced to have this pleasant companion once more with her.

CHAPTER VI

CHECKMATE

When Mr. Richard arrived in Bristol he put up at a hotel overlooking College Green; but he had no intention of going at once to Holiwell Vicarage; he wanted time to think. For indeed he was as one distracted; wild projects flashed through his brain—in a sort of restless and reckless despair; one moment he would be for confessing the whole truth to Nanciebel, and throwing himself on her mercy; the next he would be for an immediate marriage, as the one definite settlement of all these perplexities. He went out and wandered through the streets of the town, seeing hardly anything. He followed the

Whiteladies' Road until he emerged on Durd-ham Down; but the fair English landscape, all shining in the white light of the spring, brought no joy to his heart. When he ought to have been thinking of Nanciebel, and of his visit of the morrow, he was in reality wondering what his cousin Florence had said when she discovered he was gone; he was picturing her walking in the garden with the little widow; he could see her driving in to Stratford, to make her after-noon purchases there. And what was that his mother had hinted—that if in other circum-stances he had made bold to speak to Florence Kingston, he need not have feared her answer? That was not even to be thought of! How could the widow know, in any case? It was but the fond partiality of a mother. He had to turn from these fruitless and agonizing speculations over what might have been to the obvious duty that lay before him; and again and again he strove to convince himself that if he and Nanciebel were once married, there would be an end to all these hopeless and futile regrets. He had been bewildered by a brilliant and fascinating appari-tion. Nancy and her quiet ways would win in the end. The commonplace security of ordinary life was sufficient for most folk. Vain dreams, farewell!—here were peace and content, and the even tenor of one's way.

Next morning he had summoned up courage, and even formed some inchoate plans; about eleven he started off and drove out to Holiwell Vicarage. Arrived there, the housekeeper informed him that his uncle had just gone off to see some old woman in the neighborhood; that the young ladies were at their drawing lessons; and that Miss Marlow was in the garden. Accordingly, Mr. Richard replied that he would himself go and seek Miss Marlow; and presently he had stepped forth into the outer air.

He encountered Nanciebel rather suddenly— she was coming through the archway in the walk of yew—and the instant she caught sight of him she stopped, looking startled and frightened.

"What is it, Richard?" she said, when he went up to her.

And he was amazed also. She seemed to shrink back from him, as if dreading what he had to say. Yet was not this in some measure a relief? If she had flown to him with love and joy in her eyes, how could he have played the hypocrite?

"Well, I have come to see you," he said.

"Yes," she made answer rather breathlessly, and she kept staring at him with anxious scrutiny, "yes—but—but is that all?"

"I don't understand you," he made answer,

still wondering. "I—I have no bad news, if that is what you fear—nor any news, indeed."

"Oh," she said, with her face lightening considerably, "it is merely a visit? There is nothing—nothing of importance? You see," she continued, as if eager to explain, "I did not expect you, Richard—you sent no letter—and you have come long before the usual time. I was almost afraid you might have heard—I mean that there might be some bad news, or some occasion for your coming so unexpectedly. And how is your mother? It was so kind of her to send me Tennyson's last volume—to keep my set complete. Aren't the flowers here pretty?— the spring-time is always so delicious. And when are you going back to Stratford, Richard?"

He could not make Nanciebel out at all. Apparently she was most desirous to be friendly and complaisant; yet his presence seemed to embarrass her. She was nervous—constrained —her eyes watchful and furtive; this was not the Nanciebel who had clung closely to him as they walked up and down the little court-yard, under the stars. Nevertheless, he was here to perform a duty.

"Yes, I have come before the proper time, Nancy," said he, ignoring her last question, "and it is to put a proposal before you, and before my uncle. This separation that was agreed upon—well, you have complained of it before, and of your loneliness here, and I don't wonder at it—this separation has lasted long enough, it seems to me. I think if we could get everybody to agree, we might as well be married at once——"

And again she regarded him with a sort of apprehensive look, which she instantly concealed.

"Oh, do you think so, Richard?" she said in an off-hand way. "For I am hardly of your opinion. I think that an arrangement that was agreed to by everybody should be carried out; and then, you see, no one will be able to complain. It was to be a trial; and who could tell what was to happen when it began, and who can tell what may happen before it ends? For you see people are so different, Richard," continued this profound philosopher — and she seemed anxious to talk away this project into nothingness. "There are some who don't care about being petted, who are independent, and self-sufficing—and they are mostly men; and there are others who like to be petted and made much of—and they are mostly women. Very well, when there is such a difference between dispositions, isn't it wise that they should be tested by time——"

"You didn't talk that way once," said he, with

a touch rather of surprise than of actual disappointment or chagrin.

"Oh, well, perhaps not, for I was younger then," remarked this sage person; "and then being sent away from all one's friends and acquaintances was pretty trying at first. However, I don't complain now. No, I think it was wise on the part of your mother; and I am sure I thank her. And when do you go back to Stratford, Richard?"

He was completely nonplussed. Here was the sacrifice he had nobly determined to make put aside as a thing of naught; while he was practically invited to return home forthwith; and that he could not do. Florence Kingston was there—whom he dared not meet. Besides, how could he go away leaving the whole matter as it stood before, surrounded by all kinds of distracting uncertainties? It was for Nanciebel's own sake that he must persevere.

"To Stratford?" he repeated. "Well, understand, Nancy, I did not think you would agree to this without some coaxing and persuasion—and I shall have my uncle to talk over as well—so I have come down to Bristol for a little while, and I am staying at a hotel there."

"Oh, for some time?" she said, "you are going to remain here, Richard?" She was silent for a second or two. "Well, it is so sudden—so bewildering. You cannot expect me to say yes just at once, even if I knew that your uncle and your mother would consent. It is so grave a step. But—to-day is Saturday; you will give me till to-morrow? Will you come out to-morrow afternoon, Richard, and then I may be able to say something more definite? Yes, I will, I promise; to-morrow afternoon you shall have my answer——"

"But I don't want to press you, Nanciebel," he urged again; for he could not in the least understand what all this meant. "I came down to Bristol for the very purpose of talking the whole thing over, and showing how it would be better and safer and more satisfactory for every one if we could arrange for this time of probation to cease. Who knows what may happen? And you may be doubtful and reluctant, of course; for it is a grave step, as you say; but I am sure it is the best thing to do; and then there will be no further misgivings or trusting to chance."

It was hardly the impassioned pleading of a lover; but Nanciebel did not seem to look for that. She merely begged him again to give her till the following afternoon, and she appeared to be immensely relieved—and grateful—when he assented. Nor did she beg him to stay until his uncle should return and his cousins be free. She even hinted that it might be more prudent for her to say nothing of this proposal until he himself should bring it forward on the next day. In the mean time she bade him good-by with a very pleasant and affectionate look; and he returned to his hotel in Bristol, and to aimless cogitations which led to confusion rather than to any enlightenment.

But what happened next day drove away those puzzled surmises and substituted for them amazement and alarm. About half-past one o'clock his uncle drove up to the hotel, and came into the coffee-room, where Mr. Richard happened to be standing at the window. The nervous little clergyman was very much excited; but he had to speak in a low voice, for there were some people seated at the table at lunch.

"Richard," said he in a hurried undertone, "do you know what the meaning of this is? Miss Marlow has gone."

"Gone?" his nephew repeated, with staring eyes. "Gone where?"

"I do not know; she has left the house. This morning she complained of headache, and decided to remain in her own room; then when we returned from morning service, we discovered that a cab had been brought out between eleven and twelve, and that she had left, taking all her things with her. And here is a letter we found lying for you."

11

"Yes, but what did she say when she went?" his nephew demanded in blank amazement. "There must have been somebody in the house. What explanation did she give? Where did she say she was going?"

"Not a word to anybody! Perhaps you will understand from that letter," said the clergyman, looking at the enigmatic envelope.

Mechanically Mr. Richard broke the seal; he was thinking of her strange behavior on the previous day. Nor did this carefully written epistle afford him any satisfactory elucidation.

"Saturday Night.

"DEAR RICHARD: By the time you get this note, I shall have escaped from a position which was only embarrassing to you and to me, and to others. I shall always appreciate your kindness—and *never*, *never* forget it; but what you wished was *not to be*. I had intended telling you by degrees how I had come to this resolution; but your sudden appearance here to-day has precipitated matters; and to-morrow I shall take the step I have long meditated—and I am sure it will be better for us all. And I am sure your mother will be glad. I shall always remember with gratitude the sacrifices she was ready to make; and when I read 'The Miller's Daughter' I shall always think of her with respect and affection; but she did not consider, when she gave me Tennyson's poems, and hoped they would be my constant teachers, that there was another one far more applicable to my station. I refer to 'The Lord of Burleigh.' Do you remember those *significant* lines:

> "'But a trouble weigh'd upon her,
> And perplex'd her, night and morn,
> With the burden of an honor
> Unto which she was not born.'

Ah, if that poor lady had only known in time!— then she might have avoided all her misery, as I hope to do. For why should I aspire to a dignity for which I am unfitted? Your cousins here have been very kind; but all the same it has been impressed on me every day that I was not *born in the purple*. I am not ashamed of my humble origin, for

> "'Kind hearts are more than coronets,
> And simple faith than Norman blood;

but it is better for all that I should abandon a fond dream, and accept life as it is. Dear Richard, you have given me several little presents from time to time, and these I wish to return; and I will send them to you by a safe hand. If you will allow me, I will keep your photograph— for one need not forget an old *friend*, whatever trials and hardships the world may have for us.

Farewell forever, dear Richard, from your still affectionate and grateful

"NANCY.

"P. S.—I will send you the things in a day or two."

Mr. Richard handed the letter to the clergyman, but not in silence.

"Why," he exclaimed angrily, as his uncle glanced over the pages, "if that is not a piece of studied hypocrisy, it is the writing of an absolute fool! 'Born in the purple!'—where did she pick up a phrase like that?—does she consider that *I* have been born in the purple?—does she suppose that *I* was going to bestow a coronet on her?"

"Richard," said the clergyman gently, "you must remember that girls in her position like to write like that—they have learned it out of penny romances—they think it fine. I should say the letter was sincere enough, even if the terms of it strike you as being artificial. And the fact remains that she has left the vicarage."

"Precisely!" said the young man, who did not at all rejoice in the freedom that had been thus suddenly thrust upon him; for he considered that this was only some kind of incomprehensible freak on the part of Nancy, and that, after an immensity of trouble and annoyance, they would all of them find themselves precisely in the same straits as before. "And now we shall have to hunt her out, and convince her that her heroic renunciation is out of place! I suppose we shall have to advertise, 'Come back to your sorrowing friends!' Upon my word, it's too bad! We shall have all this trouble for nothing. I suppose she wouldn't go to Stratford, and confess to her relatives that she could not bear the burden of the honor that was destined for her. That would not be romantic enough! She will wait until the whole of our family go to her as a deputation, and beg her on their knees to accept the coronet!"

"You are angry and impatient, Richard," the clergyman said quietly. "But there is more in that letter than you seem to see. It has been written with deliberation; it has been thought over for some time back. It is no sudden freak. Now come away out with me to Holiwell, and we will see if we cannot find out something about this very odd affair. Gertrude and Laura may help us. And we are bound to make inquiries—until we know that the girl is in safety; she cannot be allowed to vanish into space in this fashion."

As they drove away out to the vicarage, Mr. Richard did not speak a word—his brain was busy with all manner of conjectures and wild speculations. Supposing, now, that he were to take Nancy at her word? Of her own free will she had withdrawn from the engagement which of late he had felt as a very millstone round his neck. No doubt his word was given to her; but here she had in set terms renounced her claims; and why should he not accept her renunciation? But, even as he argued with himself in this way, he felt it was all impossible. He could not be so mean as to take advantage of a fit of temper or some perverse and inexplicable whim. He knew Nanciebel; knew her contradictory moods; knew how affectionate she could be at one moment, and how petulant and wayward the next; and he could not make this fantastic letter an excuse for backing out of an engagement to which his honor was pledged. How could she mean what she said in this ridiculous message of farewell? When a girl took one of the most serious steps possible in her life, she was not likely to be quoting poetry and using sham literary phrases. Perhaps (this was his final conclusion) Nancy had been finding her life at the vicarage too dull and forlorn, and had suddenly resolved to break the monotony of it with a romantic episode.

Now, no sooner had the good vicar begun to question his daughters about this mysterious thing that had just happened, than it became abundantly evident that they knew a good deal

more than they were willing to admit.   Gertrude
looked at Laura, and Laura looked at Gertrude;
and both were mute.   Clearly they did not like
to "tell."   Nancy had been their comrade in a
measure; perhaps she had even asked them to
keep her secret; and here was their cousin Richard—how could they say anything that would
lead him to doubt the constancy of his betrothed?
And yet when the vicar, getting a bit of a clew,
began to press home his questions, it seemed as
if there was nothing for it but a frank avowal.
Gertrude, as the elder, came in for most of the
cross-examination; and at length, with many
hesitations and shy glances at Mr. Richard, and
appealing looks to her father, she allowed them
to construct what story they might out of the following fragments and hints.

Nancy had always been fond of wandering
about in the garden—particularly when Gertrude
and Laura were at their morning exercises, and
she was left alone.   She had made the acquaintance of Mr. Stapleton's head gardener—as Richard knew—a most respectable and well-educated
and well-mannered young man.   "Mr." Bruce,
as Nancy always called him, was very kind to
her, instructing her in botany, and lending her
books.   Other books besides botanical ones, too,
for Mr. Bruce was a well-read young man, and
had quite a library.   Nancy seemed to have a

great admiration for the young Scotchman. She was always talking about him and contrasting him with others. She had cut his portrait out of a horticultural journal in which it had appeared, along with a biographical sketch, and a list of all the prizes he had won. Gertrude had even ventured to remonstrate with Nancy about her partiality for this young man—seeing that she was engaged to be married to Cousin Richard —whereupon Nancy had laughingly replied that she liked to be appreciated by some one. Nancy had shown her a photograph of the gardens at Beever Towers, and pointed out the charmingly surrounded cottage which Mr. Bruce was to occupy when he left Somersetshire for Yorkshire. That the young Scotchman and Nancy were in constant correspondence, Gertrude had to admit that she knew; but she did not consider it her duty to say anything—she thought it would be treacherous, she said.

"But Bruce left Holiwell a fortnight ago!" exclaimed the vicar, breaking in upon the shy confessions.

"Yes, papa," said Miss Gertrude, "but he has not gone to Yorkshire, for I have seen him twice during last week."

"And I saw him yesterday," observed Miss Laura, with downcast eyes.

"Yesterday?—where?" demanded her cousin

Richard, who had sat silent and bewildered all this time.

"At the foot of Crossways Lane by the pond," said the younger daughter; and then she added with some hesitation, "And—and Nancy was with him."

"Really, I am more than surprised," said the vicar with unusual emphasis, "at such conduct on the part of that young man. I had always considered him a most respectable, well-bred, honorable young fellow—indeed, I had a very great regard for him, even when he and I differed in our political views; but that he could have stooped to this clandestine correspondence——"

"Papa," said Gertrude (who also seemed to regard the young Scotchman with favor, and was modestly anxious to put in this meek apology for him), "don't you think he may have been waiting for an opportunity of coming to speak to you? Perhaps he may have wished to have all his affairs in Yorkshire settled first."

"Oh, if there has been any hole-and-corner business in the affair, be sure it was Nancy's own doing!" said Mr. Richard scornfully (alas, how inconstant are the hearts of men!—had he no recollection of certain moonlight strolls up and down a hushed little court-yard—a court-yard so hushed that one could almost in the darkness

11*

have heard poor Nanciebel's heart throbbing for very joy?). "She was always for romance, and mystery, and secrecy; and I have no doubt she persuaded this fellow into concealing the whole affair until they could declare themselves married. Or perhaps they are married already?— that would be just like Nancy. And now I know why she looked so frightened when I came here yesterday——"

"Cousin Richard," said Gertrude rather piteously, "I hope you will not think I had any part in this. I could not help seeing what was going on, and perhaps I ought to have told papa, or written to you; but then I thought it would be dishonorable. Many a time I have been sorry for you, and thought you ought to know."

"Oh, but look here, Gertrude," he exclaimed, "you mustn't blame yourself at all—you mustn't imagine any harm has been done to me. Why, if what you suggest has all come true—if Nancy has gone and got married or is about to get married—that would be for me——"

But he paused and was silent. The future was vague and uncertain; these wild and dazzling hopes were not to be spoken of as yet. Nevertheless, the two girls could gather from his face that he was in nowise disappointed or depressed by this sudden news; he only insisted, in a matter-of-fact kind of way, on the necessity of getting to know of Nancy's whereabouts and immediate prospects.

He remained to mid-day dinner at the vicarage; he went with his cousins to evening service; he had some bit of supper with them later on ere he set out to walk into Bristol. And now that he had almost convinced himself that his relationship with Nancy was really finally and irretrievably broken, he began to think of her with gentleness—not with any anger or desire for revenge. She had been a most affectionate and loving kind of creature; too loving and affectionate, perhaps; she could not suffer being alone; she must have some one to cling to, some one to pet her and "be good to her." Well, well, he had nothing to reproach her with, he said to himself, as he walked along the solitary highway. When Nanciebel's soft dark eyes had looked into his, they had been honest enough at the time; it was her too tender heart that had played her false; she was hardly to blame, for how can one alter one's temperament? And he understood that letter now. It was not altogether artificial. Perhaps there was a little sentimental regret in her bidding him good-by; and perhaps she thought she could best express that in the language of books. And if Nancy wished to betray a sweet humility—or even to convey a subtle little dose of flattery—in talk-

ing of the honor of the position that had been
designed for her, why should he be scornful of
these innocent girlish wiles?   Poor Nanciebel!
She had been kind in those bygone days; he
hoped she would be happy, and run no more
risks of separation.

But he was hardly prepared for his next meeting with Nancy.   He had spent all the Monday
morning in aimlessly wandering about, discuss-
ing with himself the various possible ways and
means of getting into communication with that
wayward and errant damsel; and at last he was
returning to his hotel, about lunch-time, when
behold! here was Nanciebel herself, her hand
on the arm of a tall and rather good-looking
young fellow of grave aspect and quiet de-
meanor.

"O Mr. Richard!" said Nanciebel, with her
face flushing rosily and her eyes shining gladly,
"this is just what I have been hoping for!   I
knew we should meet you somewhere!   Will you
let me introduce my husband?—you've met before."

The two men bowed, and regarded each other
with a somewhat cold and repellant scrutiny;
which could tell how the other was going to take
this odd situation of affairs?   But it was Nancy,
with her eager volubility, who got over the awk-
wardness of the meeting.

"Yes, indeed, Mr. Richard, for I made sure you would be glad when you heard the news. I have seen for many a day that you wished our engagement broken off—I could read it in every line of your letters; but I wanted you to speak first. Then you frightened me on Saturday—did you really mean what you said?—or what was your intention? Anyway, it's all right now, and you are free; and now James and I can make any apologies that are necessary for the concealment that has been going on. Oh, but that was all my doing, Mr. Richard—indeed it was! I declare it was! James was for going direct to your uncle and explaining everything; and I said that would only provoke a tremendous family disturbance—that it would be far better for us to get married, and then no objection could be taken. Yes, we were married this morning," continued Nanciebel, with a becoming modesty, "and Mr. and Mrs. Stephens, with whom I am staying, have gone away home, and so James and I thought we might come for a little walk. I am so glad to have met you, Mr. Richard——"

But here Mr. Richard, who had been considerably flurried by this unexpected encounter, and by Nancy's rapid confessions, pulled himself together.

"But look here," said he boldly, "where's the wedding-breakfast?"

"Oh," said Nancy with another blush, "the Stephenses are to have a few friends in the evening; but I think we shall leave by the afternoon train for London——"

"Very well," said Mr. Richard, "but in the mean time? See, there is my hotel—suppose you and your husband come in and have lunch with me—let it be a wedding-breakfast, if you like. What do you say, Mr. Bruce?"

An odd kind of half-embarrassed smile came into the young Scotchman's grave and handsome face.

"I have not much experience in such matters," he answered in his slow, incisive way, as he looked at his bride with affectionate eyes; "but I should think in such a case, it would be for the young lady to say what should be done."

"Oh, then, I say yes!" cried Nanciebel in an instant. "Oh, it is so kind of you, Mr. Richard! for you know I wouldn't for the world have any disagreement or ill-feeling remain behind; and now I can write down to Stratford that you are quite good friends with us, and I hope you'll tell your mother so, and your uncle, and Gertrude and Laura. It is so very, very kind of you, Mr. Richard!" again said Nanciebel, almost with tears of gratitude in her soft dark eyes.

The improvised wedding-breakfast was a great success; and Mr. Richard played the part of host

with a quite royal magnificence. The young
Scotchman was throughout grave and self-pos-
sessed, but not taciturn; when he did speak,
there was generally something in what he said.
But indeed, it was Nancy who did all the talking; chattering about everything and nothing,
and always turning for confirmation (but not
waiting for it) to James. And then again, when
it was time for them to go, Mr. Richard accompanied them into the hall, and had a cab called
for them; and as he bade them good-by on the
wide stone steps outside, Nancy took his hand
and pressed it warmly, and looked into his eyes
almost as once she had looked, and murmured
in a soft undertone:

"You *have* been kind!"

Such was the fashion of their parting; but
Nancy's eyes were still once more turned back
to him, and she waved her hand to him as she
and her husband drove away.

Now, it was about a fortnight afterward—perhaps a day or two less—that Mrs. Kingston and
her niece Florence were in the little boudoir at
Woodend; and, strange to say, the latter was
down on her knees with her head buried in the
widow's lap, as if she had been making confession.

"And may I call you mother?" was the conclusion of her tale, uttered in only a half-heard voice.

"Indeed, you will be the dearest daughter I could have wished for," said the widow, most fervently, as she stroked the pretty hair with both her hands. "I never thought to see this day; it is everything I could have wished for, dear Florence."

"You are not angry, then?" said the fair penitent, without looking up. "But I shall never believe you care anything about me until you call me Floss."

"I will call you anything you like, my dearest," said the widow, again clasping and petting the pretty head that lay bent and humbled before her.

Then Cousin Floss arose. Humility with her could only be a passing mood. She seated herself next the little widow, and put her arm within hers.

"What do you think papa will say?" she asked.

"Well, my dear," said Mrs. Kingston, "I think I know what he will say; but if you are at all afraid, I'll go into the garden and ask him myself—this very moment."

"Will you?" said Cousin Floss, with shining eyes. "And mind you let him know that Richard has told me everything—everything. Papa knew about—about Miss Nancy, didn't he?"

In a second or two the widow was in the garden, where Uncle Alexander, with his quick, shuffling little step, was pacing up and down the measured path. She told him her story. Uncle Alexander's instant question was:

"Well, how much had you to pay?"

"I don't understand you," the widow said, truly enough.

"How much had you to pay?" the hypochondriac repeated testily (for he had been interrupted, and had forgotten where he was in his prescribed laps). "What money did you give the girl? It was my proposal originally; I must reimburse you. I dare say you gave her far too much; but never mind; I'm glad Floss is going to be taken off my hands — she worries me. What money had you to pay?"

"Why, we never offered Nancy a halfpenny!" Mrs. Kingston exclaimed, but she was far too happy to take offence. "We could not! She married a young man in a very good position, of excellent character, and with the most favorable prospects. But I will say this, Uncle Alexander," continued the widow, grown bold. "If you are generously minded about her, give me a certain sum, and I will add a similar amount; and when Richard and dear Florence go up to town with us next week, they can look about and buy something to send to—to Nancy."

"Very well, very well," said Uncle Alexander; and away he went on his shuffling pedestrianism again.

About half an hour thereafter, Mr. Richard returned to Woodend—he had been into Stratford about some small matters. ·Cousin Floss tripped off to meet him in the hall.

"Oh, Cousin Dick," said she, "do you know what has happened now?"

"Has the sky fallen?" said he. "And have you caught any larks?"

"Oh, you will be quite sufficiently surprised," she said confidently. "For papa has been told everything; and he has not cut off my head; no, his plans are quite different. Do you know the very first thing you and I have to do when we go up to town next week? We have to look about—in Bond Street, I suppose—for something very nice, and very handsome, and very useful; and papa and your mother are going to pay for it between them. But you couldn't guess what this wonderful thing is wanted for—no, you couldn't."

"What, then?" he demanded.

"Why, a wedding-present for Nanciebel!"

THE END.